GUTTED

Nicole L. Bates (signature)

NICOLE L. BATES

Copyright

*This book is dedicated to all the babies
who left this world too soon, and all the
parents whose arms ache to hold them.*

ALSO BY THIS AUTHOR

NOVELS
Gutted- you are currently reading this novel ☺

THE LERON SERIES
Empyrean (The Leron Series Book One)
Empyrean's Fall (The Leron Series Book Two)
Empyrean's Future (The Leron Series Book three)

SHORT STORIES
"Fairy Tale Redux: A short Story"
"The Mortal Years" – Published in TV Gods
Anthology released by Fortress Publishing, Inc.

CHAPTER 1

A STIFF BREEZE rippled the surface of the steel blue ocean causing tiny waves that chased each other across the water and headed straight for me. Goosebumps trailed up my exposed forearms when the chilly air contacted my bare flesh. I inhaled the scent of cold salt, fish, and lilacs. While the intoxicating smell of home filled my nostrils, my fingers deftly fileted a five pound salmon. After separating the firm, pink flesh from the scaly skin and slippery entrails, I tossed the filets into a tub of circulating sea water. I pushed the head, skin, and bones down a tube on the top left side of my work station. The guts went down a tube on the top right side. Nothing on Cliff Island Sea Farm was wasted.

A lock of chestnut hair worked its way loose from the elastic tie that attempted to bind it in place. The long copper-streaked strand curled around to tickle my pale, freckled face. I tried to brush the wayward tendril back with a shrug of my shoulder, but it refused to stay put.

Having no desire to touch my face or hair with slime covered fingers, I tried to ignore the tickle across my chin. This, of course, made me think about it constantly until I was sure it would drive me insane.

I tried to shift my focus to the ache in my lower back and the dull throb of my swollen feet. This would be my last day on the docks for at least a month. Tomorrow I would be leaving Cliff Island and heading for a new island, a human-made island. I was booked for a one week stay in the state-of-the-art medical facility which had been built on a floating ecopolis. I tried to think of it as a vacation. I tried *not* to think about the fact that I'd have to deliver a baby during my stay there.

Before the next fish swam into the holding tank, I dipped my hands in my personal salt-water sink. After pulling them out, I flexed my cold, chapped fingers in an effort to regain some feeling in my most important tools.

What will it be like to be a mom? I wondered. *Will I really be able to do this on my own?*

My thoughts were interrupted by the appearance of yet another salmon, brought up from the net pools just below the dock on which I stood. After scooping the fish out with my gill hook, I slid the air gun from my belt, pressed it to the salmon's forehead, and pulled the trigger. The bullet of concentrated air impacted the fish's fragile skull at exactly the necessary velocity for a quick and painless death. I clamped the mouth in place on my filet board and returned the hook and gun to my belt before unsheathing my knife.

Cleaning the salmon took little conscious effort. Two

years of ten hour days on the docks had firmly implanted the necessary muscle memory to complete the task without thought, though my job had grown increasingly more difficult when my fingers started to swell along with my belly. I couldn't get quite as close to the fish anymore either. My shoulders throbbed with the effort of holding my arms extended in an unnatural position.

After depositing the pieces in their respective places, I pulled my arms back and pressed my shoulder blades together to ease some of the tension burning its way down my spine.

The last fish of the day bled out on my cutting board while the sun sank slowly into the red-tinged sea. When the bell rang to announce the end of the work day, I sighed with relief. I submerged my hands in the lukewarm water of my rinse sink for a full minute before attempting to wriggle my way out of my oil gear.

"Here, let me help you, Lana." I glanced back and smiled my thanks to James Straum. He and his wife, Evelyn, had been close friends of my parents. After my parent's deaths, James and Evelyn had treated me like their own daughter.

"Thanks, James."

"Are you excited about tomorrow?"

"Well, I'm excited about staying at the hospital, watching movies and reading all day, eating eggs and tomatoes..."

James chuckled.

"Well, *I'm* excited to meet that baby."

I nodded and smiled, but my grin disappeared the moment I bent down to pull off my boots.

"You're going to be a great mom. No need to worry," James said, reading my thoughts.

"Yeah, it'll be great." I really tried to sound positive, for James' sake.

We hung our waterproof overalls on the hooks behind our stations.

"Oh, Lana, I'm just going to be on pins and needles waiting to hear from you!" Evelyn wrapped me in a quick side-hug before we passed through the big automatic doors that led to the main facility.

The doors closed behind us. I marveled at the sudden stillness, at the complete cessation of wind and noise. I took a moment to pull my hair back into a ponytail and finally scratch my chin.

"I'm headed straight to the commons," James stated, his stomach growling on cue. "You want to join us?"

"Not yet," I replied. "I need to put my feet up for a few minutes, and maybe take a shower."

"All right, but you better not leave without saying goodbye." Evelyn hugged me again and then joined James, linking her arm through his. I watched them follow the crowd to dinner. I envied them. I longed for their confidence in themselves and in each other. I wondered if I would ever have that.

The soft slip-ons I wore under my boots stuck to the smooth tile floor forcing me to exaggerate my knee lifts. I worked to pull the sticky soles from the tile, no doubt making me look even more like a duck waddling down the hall.

When I arrived at the door to my room, I held my right hand in front of the scanner on the wall and waited for it to read the ID chip implanted in the meaty part of my palm. After a few seconds the red light turned green and the rectangular silver door zipped open. The door disappeared into a recess in the wall. I stepped across the threshold and barely waited for the door to close behind me before I began to strip off my stiff, stinking sea-farm issue wardrobe.

Slip-on shoes slipped off. Socks, body suit, and sweaty undergarments all sailed straight into the mini wash-box which had been built into the wall of my room. I pressed the button for soap, and then started the extra-heavy wash cycle.

I retrieved my thick terry-cloth bathrobe from the hook on the wall and slid into the cozy warmth of the material. It barely stretched all the way around my swollen belly. Even after I'd tied the belt as tight as I could, a good draft entered through the gap below my abdomen where the sides of the robe didn't quite meet.

Finally, I padded over to my desk and sat down with a sigh of relief. The scanner on the desk read my ID and a screen materialized on the table-top before me. I tapped the icon for my e-mail. Unfortunately, it was no surprise to see fifteen spam messages and only one e-mail that I actually wanted to read. After all, my closest friends all worked within fifty feet of me all day long and were now devouring some variation of fish stew in the dining hall.

With the tip of my finger I tapped the one I did want to read, a reminder e-mail for my pick-up at the harbor at eight a.m. tomorrow. I tapped the confirmation button. The subsequent click stirred the butterflies in my stomach.

You're not due for six more days, I reminded myself. *This is just a boat ride to the mainland. No big deal.*

Next I scrolled through my favorites and tapped the link to the stats page on the Portland's Main Medical Center website.

Five more stillbirths reported today. The worldwide stats indicated that one in six live births were diagnosed with strong potential for developmental delay. One in ten diagnosed with early-onset neurological disorder.

I closed out the screen and sat back in my chair, staring up at the wall.

What will I do if my baby becomes one of those statistics?

I felt a solid kick directly in my ribs, no doubt a response to my elevated stress levels. I smiled and looked down, then pressed the spot where I'd felt the kick. I was rewarded with another firm push against my fingertips.

"You're going to be just fine aren't you," I whispered. "I'm sorry for worrying so much. I'm just scared. I have no idea what I'm doing."

I missed feeling my baby roll inside of me, of watching the impressions of hands and feet appear against my abdominal wall. The baby was too big now. He or she didn't have much room to move anymore.

The drawer to my right held a stethoscope that I'd ordered online. I pulled it out now and adjusted the eartips until they were firmly in place. I then held the diaphragm against my skin below my belly button. The whoosh of blood coursing through my body seemed so loud. It made me wonder why I couldn't always hear the sound of life rushing through my veins. It took a few seconds of sliding the smooth disc around before I heard the sound I'd been searching for, my baby's heartbeat.

For several minutes I sat there and listened with my eyes closed, reassured by the steady rhythm of my child's strong heart.

It must be so loud in there, I thought. *I wonder how she sleeps.*

I didn't actually know if I carried a boy or a girl. I'd told the Doctor that I wanted to wait and be surprised. In reality I was afraid that if I knew I would become too attached. For those couples who did manage to conceive in the first place, the rate of miscarriage was astronomical. Combined with the rate of still births, the live birth rate had neared a point of an actual state of global emergency.

Six more days before I would know if my baby would live, and then what?

One in six diagnosed with "strong potential for developmental delay". What did that even mean? How would I know if my baby would be all right?

Dr. Myers had recommended that I deliver in the new facility. She'd said my baby "demonstrated an accelerated rate of cerebral growth, which could indicate early-onset neurological disorder." The Doctor in the birth center specialized in treating infant developmental disorders.

No longer soothed by the white noise, I removed the stethoscope and turned on some music. I needed something mellow, almost jazzy but less random, and it was definitely time for that shower.

After switching the music to the bathroom speaker, I walked across my tiny apartment and entered my four foot by four foot bathroom. The lights slowly brightened to my preset levels of preferred wattage. My swollen fingers fumbled with the knot in the belt of my bathrobe, but finally managed to release the ties. The robe slid off my arms with a shrug of my shoulders and collected in a lavender pool around my feet.

Two steps carried me into the shower stall. I selected my water temperature and waited ten seconds before I felt the scalding rain fall on my scalp. Finally I began to scrub the salt and sweat away. Funny to think it was actually desalinated ocean water.

I scoured and rinsed and reveled in the heat sliding across my skin. My fears and worries seemed to rise up through the vents along with the steam. I stepped from the shower feeling like a new woman, ready to take on any challenge, maybe even motherhood.

With a deep breath I reached for my towel and rubbed myself dry. After wrapping the towel around my torso and tucking the corner in just over my left breast, I walked back into the main room and pulled out a standard issue white bra, white synthetic briefs, one of my three synthetic maternity body suits, and one pair of matching thermal socks.

Maybe I should invest in some new clothes.

Truly, I'd ceased to pay much attention to my appearance ever since Jack, my baby's father, had decided he'd experienced all he wanted of island life and disappeared, without a word, the day after I'd told him I was pregnant.

"That's okay, right baby, we don't need him. We've got each other." I tried my best to sound confident, convincing.

Once I'd dressed, I pulled my auburn hair into a knot at the base of my neck and secured it with a clean elastic band. I slid into a clean pair of shoes and waved my hand in front of the scanner to open the door.

A few people walked the halls, heading back to their rooms after dinner. The logos on their collars identified them as workers from the seaweed processing docks. We waved in passing.

The doors to the commons slid open. Noise and the concentrated scent of hundreds of unwashed bodies overwhelmed me. I walked toward the chow line, happy to have a good excuse to turn down a shot of the home brew that passed for liquor on the station. I'm pretty sure it was derived from fish broth but contained such a high concentration of alcohol that after a few sips no one cared.

Tonight's menu included salmon cakes. I took my plate of round pinkish patties and sautéed seaweed, carried it to table number eleven, and squeezed into the space beside Evelyn. Staring down at my plate, all I could imagine was the raw flesh and slippery guts I'd spent the last ten hours handling. I swallowed down my gag reflex and took a small bite.

"Hey, Lana, tomorrow's the big day! What are you going to do with all your time off?" Trevor, another dock worker, asked from across the table.

"Um, let's see, deliver and take care of a baby?" I

replied with a hint of sarcasm, but softened the words with a wink.

Trevor smiled.

"I might try it if it meant I didn't have to stand on those docks for ten hours a day," Trevor joked.

"Now, that's something I'd like to see," James retorted.

"Did you pick out a name yet?" Mark asked. Mark was two years older than me and generally very quiet. So quiet that when he moved here a year ago we weren't sure he could speak. He'd quickly proven himself to be the fastest fileter on the docks, so no one much cared about his communication skills.

"I have a list," I replied. "Three boy names and two girl names. I guess I'll wait and see which one suits."

"Well you'd better send a picture just as soon as that baby is born," Evelyn insisted. "I sure wish we had our own Doctor. I don't like you traveling all the way to some other island as pregnant as you are, or back with a newborn for that matter!"

"Don't worry, Evelyn, I'll be fine." Truth be told, the boat ride concerned me far less than the delivery.

Evelyn had never had any children, so she couldn't tell me what it was like. I'd watched a few online videos that were rather horrifying. In a few others the mom just walked behind a building, delivered her own baby, and walked home with it bundled up in a spare shirt. Neither end of the spectrum provided the comfort I sought. I tried to keep telling myself, *women have been doing this for millions of years, I'm sure I can handle it.*

Unless something unexpected happens, I mused. There

were no videos about how to handle delivering a still-born child.

A walking contradiction, that's me, I thought. *My greatest fear, next to becoming a mom in the first place, is not becoming one.*

CHAPTER 2

AFTER A FEW bites of dinner I felt full and exhausted, even more exhausted than usual.

"Hey, guys, I think I'm going to call it a night. I can't keep my eyes open."

"You gonna finish that?" Trevor asked, eyeing my plate.

I smiled and pushed the rest of my dinner toward him.

"We'll be there to see you off in the morning," Evelyn said giving my hand a gentle squeeze.

"You get some rest and call us if you need anything at all," James added.

"Thanks, I will." I turned and waved to Trevor, Mark, Flynn, and Rhonda. "See you in a week or so. Save some fish for me."

"Good, luck, Lana."

"Good luck."

"See you."

It took some doing to extricate myself from the long bench built into the long table, but eventually I managed.

I don't remember much of the trip back to my room. It's one of those events that you do so often you can't remember if you actually did it or not. Except that I must have because I ended up in my mini apartment, slid off my shoes, and crawled into bed.

The second my head hit the pillow, sleep took hold.

My alarm woke me at six a.m. the next morning. I groaned and worked my legs over the edge of the bed before pushing my bulk up into a sitting position. From my seat on the bed I could reach out and slide my finger across the power strip blinking on my desktop. The annoying blare of the alarm ceased and I sighed with relief.

I hadn't intended to be up this early. My boat wouldn't be here for two more hours, but I'd apparently been too tired to remember to turn off the alarm the night before. There was no hope of going back to sleep now. I looked longingly at my personal coffee maker, wishing desperately for one small cup. Maybe I should make a pot just so I could smell it, but I knew if it were there, tempting me, I wouldn't be able to resist. Instead I got a drink of water from my bathroom sink. My nose wrinkled. It was not even remotely satisfying, but much better for the baby, or so I'd been told. Personally, I thought that my severe caffeine withdrawal and half-comatose state would be worse for the child I carried, but what did I know.

My bags had been packed for a week, but I unpacked them and repacked them, to make sure I had everything. I added a few toiletries and my cell phone and still only managed to use up half an hour. Far too restless to sit and read, or even browse the internet, I grabbed my bags and decided to walk to the harbor.

I'd planned to take a cab from the station, but I had time to kill. Besides, I hadn't been off the station in months, and walking was another thing the books had said to do, so, I walked. I felt a little guilty leaving before I could say goodbye to Evelyn, but I would be back soon.

Cliff Island's primary harbor had been established long before the sea farm station had been built. For ease of access in the initial years, the station had been built on a peninsula which jutted out east of the original harbor and stretched out over Casco Bay.

Once I passed through the gates in the fence surrounding the station, I smiled at the achingly familiar site of the rocky coastline descending into the dark blue ocean. The blue was punctuated by vibrant green beds of seaweed which washed into shore and tangled around slate grey rocks. The technological advancements which were taken for granted on the station hadn't reached beyond the fence to change this tiny slice of the world. The post office/general store gleamed white in the early morning sun. Its newly repainted walls drew the eye like a fish to bait, but the old wooden sign still creaked on its old metal hinges. The screen door banged like a shotgun when Candace Jacobs walked out of the store with a bottle of chocolate milk. She waved before she climbed on her bike and pedaled off toward her parents' two story cape-cod, hair streaming out behind her.

Wanda and Larry Jacobs, Candace's parents, had been four years ahead of me in school. High school sweethearts who'd never left the island. They'd been married and moved into Wanda's grandparents' house after they'd graduated. They lived next door to my parents' house, which I hadn't set foot in since they'd died two and a half years ago. I envied Candace, still in the throes of her happy childhood on this peaceful Island, still confident in her belief that nothing would ever burst that blissful bubble. The gulls seemed to echo my feelings. They wheeled and cried piteously, ever hungry for something more.

My gaze turned again to the water, for it is a fact that one's attention can never stray long from water, especially a body of water as vast and ever-changing as the ocean. White sails stood vivid against the turquoise sky. The bright splotches of color that were lobsterman's buoys bobbed in the waves. The heady scent of lilacs drifted on the breeze. All of these pieces came together and filled me up, like a buoy for my soul.

The benches beyond the sidewalk were half-full of daily commuters who waited for boats or waited for passengers. Today I joined them, feeling a thrill of excitement about leaving the island. Worries aside, I looked forward to at least one week of eating all the eggs and tomatoes I wanted, and at least two weeks of not having to stand on the docks and gut salmon for ten hours a day. I vowed not to eat a single mouthful of fish, or anything that came from the ocean for that matter, during my entire stay at the hospital. I didn't know exactly how long that stay would be. It would depend on when the baby arrived, and the baby's health after delivery. I'd packed for two weeks, just in case.

The sound of the surf soothed my nerves. I rested my hands on my belly and inhaled deeply.

"Do you hear that, baby? That's the sound of home. It won't be long until we're back here. It won't be long until you're the one riding your bike to get a bottle of chocolate milk." That thought made me smile, a small but genuinely happy grin. "I think you're going to like it here."

Feeling calmer than I had in months, I watched the horizon until I saw the small white boat with the medical symbol on its hull a good ten minutes before it reached the harbor. A result of a lifetime of watching the sea, I could spot changes on the horizon as well as any sailor.

The small craft docked and I stood. A two-person crew tied the boat on while I approached the harbor master station and prepared to meet my escorts.

A young woman with a perky, perfect ponytail approached alongside a man who looked like he wrestled sharks for fun…and won.

Once I'd reached the station, I held up my right hand so that the harbor master could scan my ID through the little window. After a few seconds the light on the gate turned green and I pushed it open then stepped through to meet the people who would take me on the hour and a half boat ride to the hospital.

"Lana Wexler?" The young woman asked.

I nodded and she smiled, revealing a row of bright white teeth.

"I'm Nurse Bell and this is Rafael, our driver today. Are you all packed and ready?"

Again, I nodded, and indicated my duffel bag and backpack.

"This is it," I stated.

"All right, let's get going then." Nurse Bell turned and led the way toward the boat. Rafael fell in step behind me.

"Watch your step!" Nurse Bell had stepped lightly into the craft and now held out a hand to help me into the rocking boat.

"Thanks," I said, once safely on board.

Nurse Bell smiled, and then helped Rafael by holding a post to keep the boat from floating away. Rafael untied the ropes and tossed them on board. The muscles in his forearms rippled bunched and rolled like snakes under his skin. When he jumped into the middle of the boat, he landed lightly. The boat rocked once and then stilled.

Nurse Bell pushed us away from the dock before taking a seat across from me. The soft whir of the hydro-powered engine stirred to life. The call of the gulls could still be heard from shore, mourning the departure of the yet another potential food source.

Rafael took us slowly around the southwestern peninsula of the island. I saw my parents' house, my house now. It stood there, dark and empty, overlooking the bay like a widow who still watched and prayed for the return of the boat she knew had been lost.

Once we hit Luckse Sound, Rafael opened up the engine and steered us north, toward Chandler Cove. I pulled my windbreaker closed at the top. I couldn't zip it anymore, but the extra layer still provided a modicum of protection against the salt spray which leaped from the broken waves and splatted against my face and arms.

Goosebumps rose along my arms and I tried to pull my jacket tighter around my swollen body.

"Have you been to an ecopolis before?" Nurse Bell shouted to be heard.

"No," I shouted back.

"Well, just a second," Nurse Bell leaned over and began to dig through an oversized hand-bag which rested at her feet. She pulled out a shiny brochure with a triumphant smile and held it out to me.

I kept my fingers clenched around my windbreaker.

She shook it once in that "here, take it" kind of way before I tentatively reached out and accepted the offering.

I sat up straight so that I could shield the shiny paper from the glare of the sun. My eyes adjusted quickly and I stared at the glossy image of one of the human-made islands they'd been building all along the coastline.

Without opening the pamphlet, I looked back up and Nurse Bell and raised my eyebrows.

"You are in for a treat!" she stated with a voice full of excitement. "Construction was complete one month ago and you are one of the first people to have the opportunity to deliver your baby in this beautiful, peaceful environment with the best staff. Your baby will have access to cutting edge treatment from day one, if necessary.

Wait until you see it! It's absolutely beautiful, so much more peaceful than the city, and almost toxin-free! It's completely self-sustaining and the material that it's made with actually absorbs chemicals in the environment and leaves the island with pure air and pure fresh rain water. Once you see it, you'll want to stay forever, believe me."

My gaze traveled back down to the pamphlet. It did look beautiful.

"Will Dr. Myers be there?" I asked. "She said she might try to visit but I haven't heard from her since my last appointment."

"Oh, well, I think Dr. Ammon will be leading the delivery. He's the only OB currently on the island, but he is the absolute best! He is the leading expert in detection and treatment of early onset neurological disorders."

"Yes, Dr. Myers told me. What is the treatment?"

"He uses the latest in protein replacement therapy," she announced eagerly. "And he's been doing trials in gene manipulation!"

"In infants?" I asked, surprised I hadn't heard more about this in my obsessive research about childhood disorders.

"Well, in rats actually, and a few pigs."

I nodded slowly, not sure that I would trust a treatment that had only been used on rats and pigs.

We sat in silence while the boat pushed through Chandler Cove and back out toward open water.

"How much farther?" I asked.

"About thirty more minutes," Nurse Bell replied.

I decided to take a closer look at the brochure while I waited. It boasted a freshwater lagoon at its center which collected rain water for use on the island and served as ballast. The hospital and a large greenhouse were the two primary structures on the island. For entertainment one could look out of the underwater observatory, play a round of mini-golf on the lush grass, or take a walk on one of the myriad white walkways which circled and criss-crossed the structure. They even raised their own chickens.

It certainly looked bright and positive.

Nothing can go wrong in a place like this, I thought. *Can it?*

CHAPTER 3

From a distance the Ecopolis looked a bit like a giant football stadium rising up out of the water. Two great hills rose from the surface and curved back down gracefully, like high-rise seating for the main event. Opposite the two hills, and directly in front of the boat, a swath of flat, lush green stretched out in front of a multi-tiered cylinder which rose from the center of the island.

"That's the hospital complex," Nurse Bell announced, pointing to the rising cylinder. "The hill to the left is the greenhouse, the hill to the right is housing, covered on the outside with greenery. Eventually staff and families will be able to stay there. No one lives there now."

The hydro-powered craft slowed once we approached the southernmost of the island's four marinas. Rafael actually drove us directly into a protected dome which was part of the island.

"It even closes if there's a storm," Nurse Bell stated. Her voice echoed in the cavern. At least a dozen other boats were suspended in the air on lifts alongside elevated docks, safe from the gentle wake we created.

"That's mine," Nurse Bell said, pointing to a small, fast-looking silver speedboat.

"It's nice," I replied politely.

Nurse Bell beamed like I'd complimented her personally. I guess she liked her boat.

Rafael directed the craft alongside a dock. He maneuvered the boat slowly, carefully, back and forth until I heard a beep. He cut the engine.

A gentle whir could still be heard, but now it came from the dock. Or, more precisely, the lift attached to the dock, which rose to meet the bottom of the boat.

I gripped the sides of the boat. When the lift made contact, the boat tipped ever so slightly, adjusting itself into the padded hold. After that there was very little movement save the steady upward momentum which slowed and finally came to a smooth stop once the bottom of the boat became level with the dock.

Nurse Bell hopped over the edge with the ease and agility of a child, even managing to land light on her feet. She turned with her big, perky smile and extended a hand to help me out. I handed her my bags first, which she placed on the dock beside her, then I proceeded to heave my bulk up onto the bench seat and carefully, ever so carefully, over the edge of the boat and down onto the dock.

My heart pounded and my breath came in gasps when I finally stood safely on the dock. Rafael was the last one out. He stepped over the edge and his long legs reached the ground on either side. He never said a word and never offered to help with the bags. He simply turned and headed for what appeared to be the only entrance to the Island from the sheltered marina.

"Friendly guy," I whispered before I crouched down to pick up my bags. I couldn't bend at the waist anymore. I had no waist anymore.

"Here let me help with that." Nurse Bell took the larger of the two bags and slung it over her shoulder. I wondered if she'd be able to carry it all the way to the hospital.

"He's just not great with people," Nurse Bell explained.

"Yeah, I gathered," I replied.

Nurse Bell grinned.

"Follow me," she said.

Her smooth black ponytail swayed in a hypnotic rhythm. I followed it, and her, along the length of mostly empty dock until the movement stopped and I saw a security door close behind Rafael.

Nurse Bell set my bag down, placed her face close to the security panel, waved her hand in front of the ID scanner, and finally typed in a series of numbers that I could not see. The door opened, she hefted the bag and waved me forward.

"You won't get a passcode, since you'll always be leaving or arriving with one of us, but scan your ID here," she paused. I followed her instruction.

When the door opened, I started up the short flight of stairs toward another door. I stopped on the landing and Nurse Bell had to scoot around me to show her ID and enter her code again.

"Pretty tight security," I commented. I stepped forward for my own scan. Seconds later, the door opened to the main level.

"Yeah," Nurse Bell replied. "It's more annoying than helpful really."

"You have to do this everywhere you go?"

"Even my own room!" Nurse Bell exclaimed. "The Doctors and head of security are the only ones who can access any part of the facility they want with just a swipe of their hands."

"Sounds kind of like the station," I mused.

"Well, good, you'll be used to it then."

We passed through the door to the main level. The white sidewalks and supports gleamed in the morning sun. The lush grass looked fake due not only to its color, but the perfect uniformity of each blade. They stood straight and of equal height, not a single one straying from position.

Nurse Bell led me toward the cylindrical building in the center of the island. Rafael had disappeared. I wondered about his full job description. He must not be just the boat driver if he had access to the entire facility.

Thoughts of Rafael fled my mind once the dazzling walls of the hospital loomed above me. My stomach did a small flip-flop when I inserted myself into one wedge of the spinning entrance after Nurse Bell. I stepped into the lobby and followed Nurse Bell to the front desk. I took a deep breath in an attempt to calm my racing heart. The soft sounds of cascading water met my ears, accompanied by the low, soothing rhythm of instrumental music. A water feature in the waiting area proved the source of one of the sounds. I wondered if it used fresh or salt water.

A slender man sat behind the long curving reception desk with his elbows resting lightly on the gleaming surface, hands folded just in front of his chin. I stepped forward to stand beside Nurse Bell. The man rested his forearms on the desktop and leaned toward me, glancing from my belly to my tight-lipped face.

"Nervous, are we?" he asked, smiling a friendly smile.

"A little bit," I admitted.

"Well, don't be," the young man stated. "This is the best hospital in the entire Atlantic Ocean!"

He winked and I couldn't help but smile, then he turned his attention to Nurse Bell.

"And what can I do for you today, Lacy Bell?"

Lacy, her name was Lacy. Good to know. It suited her.

"I need to register one Miss Lana Wexler, here to see Dr. Ammon." Nurse Bell sounded very professional, but her wink to the receptionist let me know they were playing at being formal.

"Right away, Ma'am, right away."

The receptionist tapped the table-top to his right. A keyboard appeared on the desktop and a screen materialized in the air to his right. The young man tapped and slid a series of icons on the screen before reaching the one he needed.

Nurse Bell pulled a zip drive from her pocket and handed it to the receptionist.

The receptionist took the drive, uncapped it, and inserted it into a port on the edge of the desk. He began to type, his fingers flew over the keys so fast that I couldn't even begin to guess what he was typing. He would periodically lift his right hand and tap or slide the screen while continuing to enter information with his left.

"Okay, I need your ID please."

It took me a moment to realize he'd been speaking to me.

"ID," he repeated, tapping the box which had appeared on the desktop in front of me. The lines around the box flashed red and inside it read, *scan here*.

"Oh, sorry." I held my hand over the flashing rectangle until it stopped flashing. The words changed to: *tap to accept*.

"Accept what?" I asked.

"Oh, that's for me," the receptionist replied.

He tapped the box, typed more information on his flat keyboard, and finally tapped several places on his suspended screen.

"All set!" he announced before he waved his hand over the desktop again, causing the keyboard and screen to disappear.

"Thank you, Brian." Lacy Bell nodded, and then turned toward a set of clear, interior double doors.

After holding her hand in front of yet another scanner, the clear doors whooshed apart. We stepped through together and the doors closed behind us with a soft snick. The first thing I noticed was the silence. The Zen-garden ambiance of the lobby disappeared, replaced by a complete lack of sound. I actually held my breath it was so quiet. The walls and floor seemed to absorb sound before it had been made, making me feel the need to tip-toe.

Lacy Bell had only walked a few feet before she waved her hand again and opened the door of a clear elevator.

Inwardly, I cringed. I really hated clear elevators. I tried to keep my expression neutral, but I did close my eyes once the door shut. I kept a firm grip on the railing attached to the wall at waist height, bracing myself for the first stomach-dropping jolt of movement.

The soft ding a few seconds later surprised me.

"That was smooth," I said. I stepped into another hallway identical to the one we'd just departed.

Nurse Bell led the way around the corner and I gasped when I saw that nearly the whole outer wall of the hallway was lined with floor to ceiling windows. The hospital was not a closed cylinder, but actually a wheel and spoke formation, the spokes extended from one side to the other over open water below.

"That's the lagoon. Snow and rainwater are collected and purified for use throughout the island, and also fill the holds to serve as ballast," Lacy Bell explained.

"Huh," was all I could think to say.

My gaze remained fixed out the windows as we walked a quarter of the way around the circle. I nearly collided with Nurse Bell when she stopped in front of a solid panel which, I realized upon closer inspection, was a door. This door led to one of the long spokes which stretched from one side of the inner wheel to the opposite.

Nurse Bell held her hand up, but the door didn't open.

"It needs to scan both of us before it will open. You're registered now."

"Oh." I held my hand up and waited for the small red light at the top of the black rectangle to turn green. The door zipped open and I stepped into a long hallway lined with doors. My feet squeaked on the shiny floor.

"Is anyone else here?" I asked.

"Dr. Ammon should be up here in his office. There are only two other patients on this floor right now. The other floors have more but, like I said, this is a very new facility."

It smelled new, like warm plastic. There were no overpowering odors caused by too much cleaner or too many bodies in an enclosed space for too long.

"Right this way," Nurse Bell said, unnecessarily. There was no other way to go but straight ahead.

At the opposite end of the hall, Nurse Bell stopped in front of the last door on the left. She set my bag down on the floor, smoothed her shirt and her hair, and finally knocked.

I shifted my backpack from one shoulder to the other, and then shifted my feet in an attempt to ease some of the tension in my lower back, which had begun to burn. The door opened and my movements ceased. A striking middle-aged man with a sprinkle of grey in his black hair caught me with a look that made the back of my neck tingle.

In the second or two that it took for his gaze to shift from me to Lacy Bell, I felt like I'd been weighed, measured, and thoroughly interrogated.

"Dr. Ammon, this is your new patient, Lana Wexler.

The one referred from PMMC." Lacy Bell's voice seemed a bit higher than normal. When I glanced over at her, I noticed the fingers of her right hand were twisting the diamond band around her left ring finger.

Dr. Ammon nodded and then turned without a word. My shoulders immediately relaxed.

As he walked over to his desk, I finally took notice of my surroundings. Both side walls were made from single sheets of clear material which overlooked the freshwater lagoon. From this vantage point I could also see the inner curve of both sides of the main structure. The entire building seemed to sparkle in the sunlight, all white and windows. It was elegant, and beautiful. I felt completely out of place.

"Did Nurse Bell explain the nature of our program?" Dr. Ammon asked. He gazed out the window rather than making eye contact with me. Though the question had clearly been directed at me, I glanced at Nurse Bell for a clue. She cocked her head in a rather impatient gesture, indicating I should answer.

"Uh, yes, briefly," I responded, hoping that kept Nurse Bell out of trouble, but gave him leeway to tell me more if that was his intention. "But I would appreciate any information you might have. I would also like to speak to Dr. Myers. I wondered if she'd be attending me here."

It took all my courage to add that last phrase. Me, a dock worker on a sea farm which, believe me, was not the place for a woman without a backbone. I didn't understand the effect this man's presence had on me.

He turned to face me and I had to force myself not to look away.

"What else do you wish to know?" he asked.

It seemed like a simple enough question, but it felt like one of those situations where you don't know what you need to know, so how can you ask the right questions? My nostrils flared in frustration and I tamped down hard on the unease that roiled within my chest.

"I'd like to know more about the treatment, and if my baby will need it. I need to know that my baby is going to be safe." Finally, my voice sounded like my own, confident, able to hold my ground.

"You'd be hard pressed to find a safer place, for you or your child. I'm sure you've noticed that our security is top of the line and we can provide treatment that is not yet available anywhere else." Dr. Ammon's expression never changed. Nurse Bell, however, grinned like a kid on Christmas morning when he glanced at her and asked, "Isn't that right, Lacy."

"Yes sir, the absolute best treatment available."

I raised an eyebrow at Nurse Bell, and then turned back to Dr. Ammon.

"I'd still like to speak to Dr. Myers. She's the one who referred me and I'd like to know what she has to say before I agree to any treatment." I was on a roll now, feeling less intimidated with each pronouncement.

"I understand. Perhaps we should try to call her now." He cocked one eyebrow at me and I blinked in surprise.

"Yes, please, I would like that."

"One moment." Dr. Ammon released his hands,

which he'd had clasped behind his back, and closed the distance between himself and his desk. He sat in a curved-back chair and tucked himself in before sliding a hand across his desk-top.

With one long, tapered finger he tapped an icon and a screen appeared, just like the one at the reception desk. This time I noticed a light projecting from a small circle on the desk.

Dr. Ammon tapped the screen and I could see a long list of names with telephone icons beside them. He scrolled through the list until he came to the one he wanted and tapped it. I heard a faint ringing sound and after the third ring a face appeared on the screen, not one that I recognized, not that it would have been easy to determine who it was anyway with the image reversed.

"Hello, Dr. Ammon, how can I help you?" the voice of a young woman came through the speaker. I saw the lips of the flipped-faced image move. It was rather disconcerting to watch, so I kept my eyes on Dr. Ammon.

"I would like to speak to Dr. Myers if she is available."

"I'm sorry Dr. Ammon, Dr. Myers is with a patient right now. Can I take a message?"

"Yes, I have a new referral, one Lana Wexler, who was a patient of Dr. Myers's and is expecting a baby any day now. Dr. Myers referred her to my facility and Miss Wexler would like to speak with Dr. Myers at her earliest convenience."

"I will give her the message," the woman replied. "Is there anything else you need, Dr. Ammon?"

"No, thank you, Karen."

"Have a good day."

Dr. Ammon nodded and closed the window, then tapped his desk and the screen disappeared. He folded his hands on his desk and watched me.

Finally, I shrugged. I felt incredibly tired already and my back burned like someone had rubbed too much icy hot into my skin.

"All right then. Is there somewhere I can lay down?"

Dr. Ammon shifted his gaze to Nurse Bell.

"Please show Miss Wexler to her room." Then he turned back to me. "I will check on you in the morning."

I arched my back and placed both hands along either side of my spine and stretched. Nurse Bell led the way out of the office, where she picked up the bags she'd deposited outside the door, and then continued down the hall.

We made it almost halfway down the hall before she stopped and began punching numbers in a keypad affixed to the right of another door.

The door zipped open and we stepped inside. Nurse Bell entered another code on an identical panel inside the room and the door zipped closed.

"Where's the scanner?" I asked, half in jest.

"There isn't one on the patient rooms, for security. It's a little silly right now, but once the facility is full Dr. Ammon doesn't want anyone except himself or the assigned nurse to be able to go into and out of each room. It's also for the safety of your child. Babies are worth a lot now."

My hands went immediately to my distended belly, covering my child protectively. A shudder ran through me. The thought of someone stealing my baby made me kind of glad that I'd been sent here.

"All of the lights, shower, and food are either voice activated or have a pretty standard touch screen. If you need me, or you want to take a walk outside, or see the underwater observatory, you just page me by pressing this button." she pointed out a small yellow button that was part of the key pad by the door.

"Don't I get to know the room code?"

"No, sorry, it's standard policy."

"So I'm locked in here?" I did not like the sound of that at all. "What if there's a fire?"

"You'll be fine, I promise." She gave me a reassuring smile, apparently oblivious to the fact that I was, essentially, her prisoner. "Is there anything else that you need?"

"I'm really hungry," I replied. "And I really need to sit down."

Nurse Bell's soft soled shoes made a whisk-whisk sound as she walked toward the corner of the room where a table and two chairs had been arranged. Behind this tiny dining room was an equally minuscule window built into the wall.

"This is where you order your food." She tapped the screen to the right of the tiny door and dozens of icons appeared. She waved me over to take a closer look.

As I stood behind Lacy Bell, staring at the screen, my mouth began to water. Each icon depicted a plate of delicious-looking cuisine which I could order with the touch of a button.

"You touch the one you want, the kitchen gets the order, and they send it up. Want to try it?"

Nodding, I stepped forward. Nurse Bell moved to the side.

"Okay, baby, what sounds good today?" I scanned the items slowly and stopped on a picture of scrambled eggs topped with fresh salsa. "That looks amazing. Is it made with real eggs?"

"Yes," Nurse Bell replied. "We have our own chickens, lab grown of course, but as real as they come anymore. We also have our own greenhouse and, of course, plenty of fish."

My nose wrinkled at the mention of fish and Nurse Bell laughed.

"I guess you get more than enough fish working on a sea farm, huh?"

"Way more than enough," I replied. "Even the alcohol is made from fish broth."

This time Nurse Bell wrinkled her nose.

"I know, right."

"Well, you'll have lots of options here, though not in the way of alcoholic beverages, and they're all made fresh to order."

"I just push the button?"

"Yep," Nurse Bell nodded once and gestured toward the screen. "Give it a try."

Reaching out with my right pointer finger, I tapped the picture of the eggs and salsa.

Thank you for your order, Lana Wexler. I will inform

you when your meal is ready. The voice that came from the screen had a soft British accent.

"Is that a real person?" I asked. The voice hadn't sounded artificial at all.

"No, it's an AI system, but it sounds real doesn't it?"

I nodded, intrigued but also slightly creeped out by this new discovery.

Maybe ten minutes passed before I heard the voice again.

Lana Wexler, your meal has arrived, the disembodied voice announced.

I opened the tiny door and wrapped my hands around the warm dish which contained my eggs and a heaping portion of bright red salsa flecked with green and yellow. Holding the bowl like I might a priceless sculpture, I carried it to the table and cast my eyes around for a fork.

"Utensils are in here," Nurse Bell said. She pulled a drawer open behind the kitchen counter.

She withdrew a ceramic fork and held it up for me. I retrieved it with a nod of thanks and then slid into one of the two curved-back silver chairs. My stomach growled in anticipation.

"Well, I'll go and let you eat and get settled. Page me if you need anything, all right?"

I waved but didn't watch her go. My eyes were fixed on the steaming mound of eggs. I scooped my first forkful. I heard the door zip open and before the fork reached my mouth it zipped closed again.

My eyes closed and I moaned in delight when the first bite rolled across my tongue. I could taste ripe tomatoes, onions, even fresh cilantro. The chill of the vegetables were a perfect contrast to the hot, fluffy eggs.

It may have been the best meal I've ever eaten. I savored every bite, even going so far as to press the last stray crumbs of egg between the tines of the fork and lick them off before licking the bowl clean.

Once I'd finished eating I had no idea what to do with my dirty dishes. I stood and walked behind the counter where Nurse Bell had found the fork. I discovered a sink, but no soap or wash towel that I could see.

After examining the faucet from all angles, I found the sensor that would turn it on and waved my hand in front of the reflective black square. Lukewarm water flowed from the spout and I held the fork and bowl beneath the flow, scrubbing them clean with my fingers. I'd ask Nurse Bell about soap when I saw her again.

The water turned off by itself after a few seconds and there I stood, with dripping wet hands and dripping wet dishes.

"If I were a towel, where would I be?" I muttered while I scanned the surrounding area.

In an effort to conserve both water and energy, this facility does not provide towels. I apologize for any inconvenience.

The disembodied voice made me jump. The fork slipped from my hand and clattered when it hit the bottom of the sink.

"Then how do I dry the dishes?" I asked, not actually expecting an answer.

Please place your dishes on the grooved countertop to the left of the sink. To dry your hands, you will find a very effi-

cient forced-air dryer built into the countertop to your right. Place your hands in front of the vent and wait three seconds.

My eyebrows arched in surprise, but I did as instructed.

"Well, that's interesting." I scanned the room and found a digital clock on the wall that read 11:00. "It's only eleven? What am I supposed to do for the rest of the day?"

This island has a variety of entertainment options, including: a 3-D theatre, an underwater observatory, a miniature golf course, an Olympic-sized salt-water pool, or you could take a walk through the gardens.

"Uh, thanks," I replied.

The underwater observatory didn't interest me too much, I saw fish every day. I didn't think it would be much fun to play mini-golf if I couldn't see the ball beneath my protruding belly, and there was no chance of me getting into a swimsuit to test out the pool. A movie might be fun, but that meant I would have to page Nurse Bell and then follow her around, watching that perfect friggin' ponytail sway behind her. No thanks.

"Maybe I should let my friends know where I am." I paused and waited to see what the room had to say about that, but this time she remained silent.

My bags lay on the floor by the door where Nurse Bell and I had set them down upon entering the room. I picked up my backpack and walked back to the table. Resting the bottom of the pack on the tabletop, I fished through the front pocket for my cell phone.

"No signal," I announced with a sigh. "Figures."

I walked around the room taking slow steps and holding my phone up high. My eyes never left the screen as I searched in vain for a hot spot somewhere in the tiny apartment.

"Come on, just one bar," I pleaded. After my third circuit around the room and even a desperate stroll through the bedroom and bathroom I was forced to accept that I could not make phone calls, or send e-mails, or check my accounts. I cursed softly then added, "I would have had a signal in Portland."

Since it was no longer of use to me, I slid the phone back into my pack and walked over to the desk, which stood across the room from the small dining area. The desktop had the black, reflective surface of a tabletop computer and had been situated in front of a matching panel on the wall. I pulled up a chair and waved my hand over the top of the desk.

Nothing happened.

I held my hand steady over what had to be the scanner, but no keyboard appeared, no screen popped up in the air in front of me.

"Why isn't this working?" I muttered.

We are still in the construction phase. The guest computers are not yet on-line. I'm sorry for the inconvenience.

"You've got to be kidding me."

Frustrated and anxious, I paced the room for a full twenty minutes until I couldn't take it anymore. I paged Nurse Bell.

Her company would, at the very least, be a step up from the disembodied voice of my cell.

CHAPTER 4

By the time Nurse Bell arrived, I really needed her. While I stood by the door, pressing the pager button, moisture began to ooze down the insides of my thighs. It almost felt like I was urinating, but without the preceding sensation of having had to go. It took a few seconds for me to realize what was happening.

I admit, I started to panic a little. I pushed the button again and then leaned in close to the keypad.

"Uh, hello? Nurse Bell? Dr. Ammon? If you can hear me, I think my water just broke."

Silence.

With the tips of my fingers I pulled my pant legs away from my skin. The wet feeling extended and expanded.

Should I go to the bathroom or wait for Nurse Bell? I wondered, and then I realized it did me no good to wait. I didn't have to, couldn't in fact, let anyone in the room. I waddled to the bathroom holding my pant legs and pulling them in toward each other in an attempt to keep the wetness away from my skin. Thankfully, it was a very short walk.

I stripped off my pants and underwear and began to feel twinges of pressure across my lower pelvis. Taking deep breaths in an attempt to stay calm, I used the dry part of my pants to wipe myself clean. I let out a frustrated growl when I realized that all my clean clothes were in my bag, which was back in the living room.

"Lana? Hello?" I heard Nurse Bell's voice and felt a wave of relief that someone else had arrived. Someone who knew what she was doing.

"In here!" I called, though I don't think it would have taken her too long to find me in the three-room suite.

"Lana, is everything all right?" Nurse Bell's voice came from the other side of the bathroom door now.

"Uh, I think my water broke," I replied.

"Oh! Well, are you having any contractions?" she asked.

"There are, sort of, twinges once in a while, but they don't really hurt. Aren't they supposed to hurt?"

"Eventually they'll become more intense, yes, but how long it takes to reach that point is different for every-one. Are you almost done in there? Or do you need some help?" After her initial exclamation of surprise, her voice changed and became all business. I actually felt my heart-beat slow in response to her confident tone.

"Actually, I need some clean pants, and underwear. Could you bring me my bag from the other room?"

"You won't want to have pants on to deliver a baby, honey. There are gowns in the top right drawer under the sink in there. Slip one of those on and I'll take you straight to the delivery room."

I groaned aloud when I opened the drawer and pulled out a thin, one-piece gown which I knew would drape in a completely unflattering way from neck to knee, but not actually hide anything. What I did not know was how to get the thing on. I never knew which way they were supposed to go. After trying it with the flap in the back, and discovering that I could not reach the tie, I switched it to flap in front and tied the side and flap strings together as tightly as possible.

Finally, I opened the door and faced Lacy Bell.

"Okay, let's get you down to the birthing suite. Can you walk or should I go get a wheelchair?"

"Seriously?"

Nurse Bell widened her eyes and then gave me a *just answer the question* look.

"Uh, I think I can make it down the hall."

"Okay, follow me."

Nurse Bell kept a loose grip on my upper arm as she marched through the bedroom and living room, and then opened the main door.

Once we were in the hallway, she turned right, back toward the entrance we'd first come through. We walked slowly past two, and then three closed doors. All I could think about was how much I hated it when Doctor's offices made you walk around in those stupid flimsy gowns. I mean, there we were, on an entirely human-made, self-sustaining island and I still had to walk down the hall in some half-open see-through dress and fuzzy socks with sticky tabs on the bottom. Why hadn't someone come up with a better design by now?

"Here's the delivery suite. Please hold up your hand so it can scan you in." Nurse Bell's announcement interrupted my mental tirade. Looking back over my shoulder I realized we'd only gone about four doors down from my room.

After I held my hand up for a count of three, the door zipped open. Nurse Bell led the way into a spacious and very sterile-looking room.

"Dr. Ammon will be with us shortly," Nurse Bell said. She bustled around the room, pulling items out of drawers and placing them on a tray which hung suspended from the ceiling by a long, jointed mechanical arm. The tray followed her when she moved from one end of the room to the other, suspended by an unseen force from the ceiling.

"What about Dr. Myers? I haven't had a chance to talk to her yet. Has Dr. Ammon spoken to her? Will he let her know I'm having the baby?"

"I'm sure that Dr. Ammon will notify her as soon as your baby is delivered." Nurse Bell paused by my side and gave my hand a reassuring squeeze. "Try to relax, everything is going to be all right."

"What about my friends. My phone doesn't get a signal here, and the computer in the room wouldn't let me check my accounts. No one knows where I am." My throat began to tighten and panic began to work its way from my pounding heart down to my twisting stomach.

"Lana, I need you to calm down. It's not good for you or for the baby if you get too agitated."

Just then my whole abdomen pressed inward, like a vacuum pump had turned on inside of me and pulled.

"That was definitely a contraction," I stated once I'd caught my breath.

"Good," Nurse Bell replied, not even glancing over. "We want to do things as naturally as possible, so it's good that the harder contractions are starting already. Keep walking around the room, or you can sit on that ball in the corner for a while. Just don't stay sitting too long. It's important to keep moving."

With one arm wrapped around and under my belly and the other on the wall for support, I paced the width of the room opposite the wall that was covered in dials and screens. Every five or six minutes I had to stop and breath in long, slow exhalations. My entire torso seemed to turn into a vice which squeezed the air right out of me.

"Here, let's try the ball for a little while." Nurse Bell rolled a big rubber ball over to me and spread a towel across the top. I clung to her arms as I sat down and sighed in relief.

"If you rock a little bit and do your best to relax and work with the contractions, it will open up your pelvis. The baby will come a lot easier if you don't fight against your body."

"Easy for you to say," I growled, but the ball actually did help relieve some of the pressure on my back. I tried rocking a little while Nurse Bell pressed a few small, sticky circles to my back, abdomen, and chest before she returned to the other side of the room.

"How's the baby?" I glanced up when the deep bass of a male voice interrupted my concentration.

Dr. Ammon had entered the room and stood now beside Nurse Bell, staring at the myriad of monitors.

"They're both doing very well. I've got her hooked up to the wireless monitor so you can take a look."

Dr. Ammon nodded and then turned toward me. I had to blink hard to keep him in focus as he strode across the room. He stopped a few feet away and squatted so that we were on eye level.

"How are you feeling, Miss Wexler?"

I met his eyes and gave him my fiercest glare. All of my inhibitions had fled and I now existed in a very primal state of instinct and survival.

"Like I'm having a baby," I replied in a flat voice. The corner of his mouth might have twitched in amusement, but I couldn't be sure I closed my eyes and breathed through another contraction.

Without another word Dr. Ammon rose and returned to the monitors. When I opened my eyes again I saw him tap one of the screens. I gasped when I saw a three dimensional image of a head-down infant rotate in mid-air inches away from his face.

"Is that my baby?" I stood and felt another gush of fluid coat my inner thighs.

Nurse Bell hurried over to give me her arm. I leaned heavily and held on with both hands. My grip on her shoulder was so tight that I heard her suck air through her teeth.

"Sorry," I apologized. I loosened my grip and then shuffled across the room.

"That's my baby," I breathed when I'd reached Dr. Ammon's side. I stopped and stared in amazement at the suspended image. "She's beautiful."

CHAPTER 5

THE CONTRACTIONS CAME faster and harder shortly after I'd had my first glimpse of my baby girl. Nurse Bell helped me onto the bed, which already had the back propped to about a sixty degree angle. I moaned my way through what Nurse Bell called the transition period, certain that I was not going to be able to do this. Once I was able to start pushing, everything changed.

Time became meaningless. My entire world was ruled by the demands of my body. I wouldn't have known or cared where I was or who was there, all I knew was: push, relax, repeat. I didn't count the number of pushes, I have no idea how long it lasted, but I knew without a doubt the moment I was done.

My body released its hold on my brain the moment I completed the final push. My muscles seemed to deflate from exhaustion and I slowly became aware of my surroundings. It felt strange but good to once again be able to process the words that were being spoken around me.

"She's just beautiful, Lana." Nurse Bell smiled at me and then whisked away bloody sheets with impressive efficiency. "You did great."

"Where is she?" I demanded and turned my head to find her.

"Doctor's got her right over there. He's just doing a couple of quick measurements."

"I want my baby."

A wail pierced the quiet of the room and tore at my heart.

I pushed myself up on my elbows and saw Dr. Ammon holding a cotton swab to the base of my daughter's heel.

"What are you doing? What did you do?"

Dr. Ammon scraped away the bead of blood which had formed on my daughter's heel with a tiny stick that was flat on one end and then placed a tiny bandage over the spot before he wrapped her up and brought her to me.

"I had to take a small blood sample to get our initial readings. Remember, we're here to help you and your baby." He paused and then held her out to me. His eyes seemed to shine with excitement, like what I would expect from a new father, and it seemed so out of character that I stared for several seconds before I finally held out my arms to receive my baby girl.

Tears filled my eyes the moment I saw her face. A shock of strawberry blonde hair poked out from beneath the blanket. Her eyes were dark blue. I'd read that every infant's eyes were dark blue at birth and would eventually change to their permanent color but I hoped they didn't change. The color reminded me of the sea.

I tucked my girl to my chest and shifted the flap of the gown so that she could nurse. When I rubbed her cheek she immediately turned and latched on to my nipple. I could have watched her for hours. She fell asleep quickly though, and I covered back up, content and feeling rather sleepy myself.

"Can I see her?"

I turned my head and was surprised to find Nurse Bell still in the room. A quick scan revealed that Dr. Ammon was gone.

"Of course," I replied softly, keeping my voice low so as not to disturb my sleeping child. I shifted my arm slightly so her face was more visible. Her cheeks looked rosy now that she was warm and fed. Her full lips were parted slightly and formed a perfect O.

"Oh, she is gorgeous," Nurse Bell whispered. "She looks exactly like you."

I beamed and my opinion of Lacy Bell jumped significantly in that moment.

We oohed and aahed over my daughter for another minute before Nurse Bell excused herself.

"I'm going to see if the Doctor needs anything. I'll be back to check on you soon. Here's some food and a drink if you feel up to it," she said. She maneuvered a tray next to my bed. "If you need me, just holler, I'll hear you." She tapped a silver disc clipped to the collar of her scrub shirt before giving me one last smile, and then she left. I was alone with my daughter.

I watched her tiny sleeping face and listened to her quiet breath. I was amazed by the overwhelming love I already felt for her. It felt like a switch had been flipped that made all the doubts and worries disappear, all that remained was an intense need to take care of my precious, helpless child.

"I guess you're going to need a name, huh."

I'd kind of been avoiding that part. I did have a list of options, but I hadn't been able to decide. Picking a name for a person that I hadn't met which would potentially define her for the rest of her life had felt like a pretty huge responsibility. Now that she was here in front of me, it didn't seem quite so impossible.

"Well, you don't look like an Abby, or a Mary...what about Ella?" I paused and repeated the name in my mind several times as I looked at her. "Ella Jane Wexler."

With a smile and sense of relief, I nodded and said, "I think that's the one. Hello, Ella Jane."

For a long time, I simply watched my daughter sleep. The silence was so complete that I could hear the rhythm of Ella's breathing. Several minutes later, the zip of the door opening startled me.

Nurse Bell had returned, with a wheelchair.

She smiled and whispered as she approached my bed. "Sorry, I didn't mean to wake you. I just wanted to let you know we could return to your room if you wanted to, if you think you'd be more comfortable there."

"Either way it doesn't really matter to me. What I would really like to do is contact my friends, let them know that Ella is here and that she's perfect."

"Ella? That's what you named her?"

I nodded and added, "Ella Jane Wexler."

Nurse Bell grinned and nodded as she gazed down at Ella.

"I like it, and it suits her." She looked back up at me. "You said your phone doesn't have a signal?"

"Right, and the computer in the room wouldn't let me log on."

"Well, I don't have my phone with me, but I'll go get it, then come back and take you both to your room. Once we get you settled, I'll download the contacts that you want to notify. I can send them a quick message from the computer in my room and tell them that you and Ella are doing great, how does that sound."

"That would be great. Thank you so much, Lacy."

"No problem. Before I go, are you feeling okay?"

I nodded.

"Do you need anything else?"

I shook my head.

"Okay, give me maybe twenty minutes, then I'll be back and we'll get you to your room."

Nurse Bell left and I decided to try a little of the food she'd placed on the tray earlier. I shifted Ella so that I could reach the glass of water. Droplets had beaded on the outside of the glass and the cup was still chilly to the touch when I lifted it to my lips. A refreshing gulp of cool water washed the sticky feeling from my mouth and soothed my throat, which was sore from the grunting and straining of labor.

My whole body was exhausted beyond anything I'd ever experienced before, but my brain seemed to be stuck in some kind of primal state of hyper-vigilance. Even if I closed my eyes, I had no chance of falling asleep.

I did my best to relax and not think too much. I clung to the warm, solid bundle that was Ella. My only known was that she and I belonged together. As long as we were together, everything else would be okay.

CHAPTER 6

Nurse Bell returned as promised. She held Ella and cooed at her while I eased myself into the wheelchair she'd provided. This time I was grateful for the assistance.

Once I'd settled in the seat, she handed Ella back to me and proceeded to wheel us out of the delivery room and down the hall toward my personal suite.

"Is there anyone else staying here?" I asked. "Any other patients I mean?" My voice seemed small in the long, empty corridor.

"There's one other woman here now. She actually delivered in Portland, but came here for her baby's treatment. There's another woman scheduled to arrive in two days. Kind of slow so far, but that's good for you, it means I have lots of time to take care of you and Ella."

Nurse Bell parked me in front of the door to my room before she entered the access code. I tried to watch her movements in order to decipher the pattern and guess the numbers that she pressed, but her fingers moved too fast.

The wheels of the chair created a smooth rhythm of sound as they rolled across the main floor of my suite toward the bedroom. Nurse Bell placed Ella in a small basinet which attached to the side of my bed. I worked on shifting myself from the chair to the mattress.

The soft foam displaced in response to my weight. I eased into a comfortable position, and then it formed itself back around me like a full-body hug. I sighed in contentment.

"Thank you, Lacy."

"Before you fall asleep, let me get those contacts from you."

"Oh, right," I said. I began to push my torso up off the mattress, but Nurse Bell placed a hand on my shoulder and gently eased me back down.

"Just tell me where the phone is, I'll get it."

I nodded, happy to lay back down and fighting to keep my eyes open.

"Front pocket of the backpack," I directed.

Nurse Bell's soft soled shoes scuffed across the floor and I heard her rustle through the backpack, then return to the side of the bed.

"Okay, hold up your hand."

I did as directed and Nurse Bell held my phone close to my palm so that the sensor could scan my ID.

"All right, contact list, open, you have a favorites list, a friends list, a Portland list, and…a bunch of other lists. Which ones do you want me to download?"

"Uh, just the favorites for now," I replied. "I'm sure they'll spread the word, and Dr. Myers is on that list."

My words slurred slightly. I began to lose the battle with fatigue.

"One minute, and, got 'em," Nurse Bell announced. "I'll let them know that Ella has arrived and that mom and baby are both doing well. Anything else you want me to say?"

With my eyes closed, I shook my head, which served to burrow my face deeper into the soft pillow.

"Okay, there's a call button on your nightstand. Press it if you need anything."

"Mmm-hmmm," was the best I could manage.

I never even heard her leave. I had already slipped into the peaceful embrace of sleep.

A snuffling, snorting sound woke me from my dreamless oblivion what seemed like moments later. I spent several seconds trying to figure out what could possibly be making such a sound while I simultaneously tried to convince my eyelids to open. They made it about halfway before reality clicked and I pushed myself up, wide-eyed, adrenaline surging.

Ella wriggled inside her little cocoon, head turning to the side. She began to scrunch her face and fuss.

After propping several pillows up behind me, I reached for Ella and pulled her close to me. My back settled into the wall of pillows before I lifted one flap of my gown and rubbed Ella's closest cheek. She immediately turned toward the caress and found what she'd been looking for. She latched on with surprising strength for one only a few hours old.

Her whole body relaxed once she began to suck. Ella

did her best to draw milk from my still-dry breast. A heavy, prickly feeling worked its way through my chest. Even though I knew she would get some colostrum which, according to the books was sufficient nutrition for the first day or two, I couldn't help but worry. Everything I'd read said it would take anywhere from one to three days for my milk to come in. Wouldn't she be starving by then?

I glanced up at the digital wall clock and was shocked to realize that two hours had passed since Nurse Bell had brought us back to our room.

"So, that's how it's gonna be, huh?" I whispered.

I'm sorry, I did not hear your question.

The voice of the room startled me, and Ella stopped sucking for several seconds in response. She soon resumed though, apparently deciding that all was well.

I tipped my head back against the pillows and closed my eyes, hovering in a sort of half-awake state while Ella nursed herself back to sleep.

The lethargic wheels in my brain began to turn, cranking out random questions. *When am I supposed to change her diaper? How will I know what she wants if she can't talk? When do babies start to talk? What will her first word be? Probably fish.*

I'd read everything I could get my hands on about pregnancy and delivery, but I'd never really thought about what happened next. Where were the books that told you what to do once you took the baby home?

The faint zip of the main door opening alerted my protective instincts. I lifted my head and watched the door to my room. My heart began to pound.

When the door opened, revealing Nurse Bell and her perky ponytail, I sagged in relief. Who else would it have been?

"How's she doing?" Lacy whispered, nodding toward Ella.

"Good," I whispered back.

She'd fallen asleep again, so I gently detached myself and covered up.

"Dr. Ammon would like to run a few tests. I need to take her to him, just for a few minutes." Nurse Bell reached out, but I hugged Ella close.

"She just fell asleep," I protested.

"He only needs to take a few measurements. It shouldn't disturb her."

"I want to go with her."

"She'll be fine. I'll take good care of her and you need to rest. You shouldn't be moving around too much yet." Nurse Bell looked at me with her big, innocent eyes and nodded encouragingly. "I sent out a few e-mails to your friends. Several of them replied already, congratulating you. They said they couldn't wait to see a picture." Nurse Bell smiled down at my sleeping daughter and my determination cracked.

"Ten minutes," I demanded.

"Probably less," she replied.

Reluctantly, I held Ella out so that Nurse Bell could take her. My ears strained to hear every sound as Lacy left the bedroom and walked across the main floor. When the door to my suite zipped open and then seconds later zipped closed again, I began to cry.

It was all I could do to swallow my rising panic. I swung my legs over the edge of the bed and stood, only to feel a gush of blood between my legs and a sudden dizziness which forced me to sit back on the mattress.

I trust Nurse Bell. I trust Nurse Bell. I repeated this over and over in an effort to keep myself from going crazy. The problem was that I didn't trust Dr. Ammon.

My next problem was that I really, really needed to pee.

I waited until the dizzy spell passed, then tried to stand again, but this time very slowly. I felt like an old, crippled woman. I inched my way up, one hand braced against the wall. Blood oozed slowly onto the pad in my underwear, but my head stayed clear. I worked my way slowly across the room.

Sweat beaded on my forehead. I covered the last few feet and finally sat with a sigh of relief on the toilet. I began to urinate and then immediately tensed and hissed. It burned. I spent several seconds debating whether or not to continue, though I knew, ultimately, I had no choice. My teeth clenched as I relaxed my bladder and found myself sweating in response to the pain. Then I had to rinse. Nurse Bell had told me I had to use the squeezy bottle of water to clean myself after I used the toilet. So I did, only to discover that it hurt like hell, too.

Well, that's something they left out of the books, I thought when the agony finally ceased.

I changed the pad in my underwear before pulling them back on, then stood and shuffled over to the sink. I splashed some cold water on my face and cursed the lack of towels. I had to keep my eyes squeezed shut while I stood in front of the forced air dryer and let it evaporate the moisture from my skin.

Finally, I turned and braced myself for the journey back to the bed. I heard Ella cry at the top of her tiny lungs. My breasts began to tingle in response to her cry. I slid my feet as fast as I could across the room and opened the bedroom door.

"What's wrong? What did he do?" I demanded, reaching out for my daughter.

"He did a quick scan to chart her cerebral growth and took another tiny blood sample, that's all." Nurse Bell explained as she handed Ella to me. "Ella did great."

"I wouldn't call waking her up and making her scream 'great'," I shot back, then immediately regretted my harsh tone. It wasn't Lacy's fault. "Sorry," I said and then returned to the bed with Ella. "I just don't trust Dr. Ammon."

"Oh, but he's brilliant!" Nurse Bell insisted.

"Brilliant or not, he's not so good with people." I opened a flap of my gown and put Ella to my breast. She latched on and sucked with such intensity that I winced. "I deserve that, I know. Sorry baby girl."

When my attention returned to Nurse Bell, I found her staring out the window, twisting a rather significant diamond ring around her finger.

I cocked an eyebrow and considered asking her what she was thinking about, but I didn't feel like I knew Lacy Bell well enough to get into something that personal.

"Well, I'd better go. I need to get some rest. Sorry

about Ella." Nurse Bell backed out of the room as she spoke, then turned and was halfway to the main door before she called back, "Buzz me if you need anything!"

I just waved, knowing she couldn't see me, but not wanting to shout and disturb Ella now that she'd calmed down.

"From now on you're not going anywhere without me, I promise," I whispered into Ella's ear. Her eyes opened a bit wider at the sound of my voice, but quickly resumed their half-lidded droop of contentment. I inhaled the scent of her and my heart filled beyond anything I ever could have imagined.

"At least one good thing came out of the mess I made. I'm going to do better from now on, okay?"

Ella's eyes closed and her lips opened. She was so innocent, so trusting, and so dependent on me. That moment changed me forever. In that moment the world shifted. It no longer revolved around me because now there was someone far more important than me, someone who needed my love and my protection. She became my world.

For the next three days I got no more than two hours of sleep at a time, ever. Ella nursed, slept, and pooped except for the times when she nursed, pooped, and then slept.

Nurse Bell showed up periodically to check on us or take us to Dr. Ammon's lab. At first he seemed indifferent to my presence, but then he began to take small blood samples from me "for comparison" he said.

Nurse Bell informed me that I'd received congratulations from all of the friends she'd e-mailed and they all asked to see a picture. I told Nurse Bell to wait. I wanted to be able to do that myself.

Ella's routine became my own, my confidence grew, though my need for sleep interfered sometimes with the joy of being a parent. Though I still worried about doing all of it on my own, I looked forward to going home. Every morning I woke up, feeling certain this would be the day we would return to our own little island, and every morning there were more tests.

On the seventh morning of my stay, the main door zipped open and I didn't even glance up from changing Ella's diaper.

"Good morning, Lacy," I called from the bedroom. The door was open and I knew she could hear me, but she didn't respond.

Once I'd secured the sticky tabs and snapped Ella back into her footie pajamas, I did look up. I gasped.

A man stood in the bedroom doorway, one I did not recognize. Immediately I scooped Ella into my arms and took a step back.

"Who are you?" I demanded.

"Nurse Gupta," the man replied, his deep voice at odds with his bony frame. He looked very young.

My eyes narrowed and I asked, "Where's Nurse Bell?"

"She had to return to Portland."

A feeling like ice water being dumped over me spread across my skin. Goose bumps rose on my arms.

"How long will she be gone?" I asked.

"I do not know, I am just the replacement."

Ella began to squirm and snort, which was what she

did right before she started to cry for milk. I sat on the edge of the bed and half-turned. I shifted the flap of my nursing shirt and unclipped one side of my bra. I suddenly felt very self-conscious about nursing Ella, or, more to the point, exposing any part of myself in front of this stranger.

"Why are you here?"

"Dr. Ammon asked me to bring the child for more testing."

"The child's name is Ella and she's had enough tests." My esses all came out more like hisses, I guess that's why they call it spitting mad. I tried to slow my heartbeat, but I didn't think I could tamp down the feelings that were rising within me.

I'd endured my forced stay up to this point because, well, I'd had no choice, and I had to find out if Ella needed the treatment. Dr. Ammon never said that she had a neurological disorder, or any related problems, but he was still testing. It came as a shock to realize that Lacy Bell was what had made it all bearable. She'd made me feel like someone here was on my side, like things would be okay. What would happen now?

Nurse Gupta swallowed hard enough that I could see his protruding adam's apple pull up high and disappear under his chin before it bounced back into place. His eyes shifted to the floor before meeting mine again, hesitantly.

So he felt uncomfortable also. Good.

"These tests are very important Miss Wexler. Dr. Ammon can determine, by tracking the number and extent of neural connections combined with the rate of cerebral growth in the first weeks which children are at risk for a variety of developmental disorders. The earlier the treatment starts, the better the prognosis. You want your child to receive the treatment if she needs it, don't you?"

I'd heard all of this before, and my resolve melted every time I thought of something being wrong with Ella.

"Weeks?" I repeated. "So, a few more days of this and then I can go home?"

"If she doesn't require treatment, I would say yes, though I am not at liberty to make such decisions on my own."

Tears had formed in the corners of my eyes. I turned my head and tried to blink them away.

"All right." I waited for Ella to finish nursing then tucked myself back in before transferring her to my shoulder to be burped. Something else that Nurse Bell had taught me. I hadn't known that babies needed to be burped every time they ate.

As I stood and walked out the door, Nurse Gupta stared, apparently unsure what to do next. I paused and turned back to face him.

"Aren't you taking us to Dr. Ammon?"

"I am only supposed to take the child," he replied.

My face pinched into the meanest scowl I could muster. "I'm going with her."

Nurse Gupta swallowed again. He hesitated, but finally walked past me and opened the main door.

I followed him to Dr. Ammon's lab, quite familiar though I was with the route by this time. Dr. Ammon's jaw clenched and his lips pressed together to form a thin line when he saw me step into the room, but he did not say anything.

Nurse Gupta stepped out of the way and I walked to my usual chair.

The tension in the room was palpable. No one spoke for a full ten minutes. Even Ella must have sensed it, because she began to squirm and snort even though she'd just been fed.

I cooed soothing words to my daughter while Dr. Ammon hooked up his monitors and head bands. Once he'd finished he stood in front of his wall of screens and stared for what seemed like hours. I sang songs, I wiggled my fingers, I did everything in my very limited repertoire to keep my newborn daughter happy and distracted.

A three-dimensional image of Ella's brain hung suspended in the air in front of Dr. Ammon. Different parts of her brain would light up periodically, and I noticed that the lights changed depending on what I did. When I sang, one part turned green. When I let her grip my finger and rubbed the back of her tiny hand, a different part turned blue. I was fascinated in spite of my irritation.

Then Dr. Ammon came at Ella with a needle.

"What is that?" I asked. I simultaneously moved to shield my daughter with my body.

"I need to see how her brain responds to certain chemical combinations." Dr. Ammon explained.

He seemed eager, a little too excited in my opinion about injecting some "chemical combination" into my daughter.

"Absolutely not," I replied. "I was told you needed

to monitor her cerebral growth, not her response to chemicals."

"This is part of the process. I need to determine whether or not her system can eliminate environmental pollutants and how her brain responds to them in order to see if her central nervous system is functioning in a neurotypical pattern."

"You will not inject my daughter with *pollutants*."

"Miss Wexler, it's a miniscule amount, less than she would be exposed to by breathing the air in Portland, and it's absolutely necessary to determine whether or not early treatment is indicated."

"So, what if her system can't eliminate what you inject into her? Won't that *make* the treatment necessary?"

"Not in and of itself. As I said, the amount is less even than what she would be exposed to on an average day on the mainland. It will not harm her, it will simply allow me to see, through the 3D imaging, exactly what parts of the brain respond and how her system deals with it."

"How can you be sure it won't harm her? She's only a week old!"

"This is my life's work. I can tell you with certainty that what I am doing will help her, not hurt her."

My hands actually began to shake. I had no idea what to do and I wished desperately for Nurse Bell. Part of me really wanted to let Dr. Ammon complete his testing. Part of me really wanted to know the results, but a bigger part of me felt like a wild animal, ready to tear apart anyone or anything that came close to my daughter with any kind of sharp object.

"I can't let you do this right now, I just can't. Maybe when she's a little older, or maybe if the brain measurements seem off when you check them tomorrow. I'm sorry, I just can't."

Dr. Ammon didn't respond, but he did back away and return the syringe to the tray he'd taken it from. No trace of emotion remained on his face. All the inappropriate eagerness had been replaced with a cold, business-like countenance. He removed the monitors and bands from Ella's body and then addressed Nurse Gupta, who had never taken more than two steps into the room.

"Take her back to her room. We'll check again tomorrow."

I scooped Ella up and hugged her to my chest. I could smell that she needed to be changed. Perhaps that was the reason for her fussiness.

My nerves felt frayed and I lacked the energy to do anything but sit on the couch and stare out the window after I'd changed Ella and nursed her once again. I felt exhausted but wired at the same time, an odd combination that seemed to drain my will, or at least my ability to focus.

When Ella woke again sometime later she stared up at me with her infant-blue eyes. Her features blurred when hot tears filled my own eyes before streaming down my cheeks. I just held her and cried for a while, until she began to join me. Then the time for grieving was over. It was time to take care of my daughter.

With the side of one hand I brushed away my tears and started the hourly game of what does Ella need? I tried nursing her but for once she wasn't interested. I changed her diaper even though it was barely wet. Then I walked around and bounced her for a while, which finally seemed to calm her down.

It did nothing for me though. I worried and wondered and dreaded tomorrow. What if Dr. Ammon told me her measurements were off? What if he said he had to continue his testing? And what would I say? Maybe this was the whole reason we'd been brought here. Maybe Ella would need the treatment and if he told me she needed it, how could I say no? I couldn't. Which meant I would have to watch her be poked and prodded and measured and messed with for how long?

At one point in my continuous circuit around the room, I stopped and swayed back and forth, staring down at the impossibly blue lagoon at the center of the island.

I had to trust that the Doctor knew what he was doing. I would be with her every step of the way, no matter what happened. She would be fine.

She had to be.

CHAPTER 7

IN THE DARK of the early morning I woke with a start. Immediately, I turned to check on Ella and my gasp of air stuck in my throat before it became a half-strangled cry.

Ella was gone.

Frantically, and foolishly, I looked all around the bed, checked under the covers, even looked on the floor. It seemed a little ridiculous, she couldn't roll, or hardly even scoot, but I didn't know what else to do. I couldn't fathom anyone entering my room without my knowing, so where could she have gone?

When I paused in my search to scan the room, I heard the faint snick of the main door as it closed.

All the heat seemed to drain from my body in an instant, leaving me trembling with cold rage and fear. I rose to my feet and marched into the main room only to find it empty.

With determined strides I crossed the room and stopped at the main door. I jammed my thumb against the pager button and leaned close to the speaker, determined to be heard.

"My baby does not leave this room without me! Do you hear me Dr. Ammon? Bring my baby back Right. Now!" Deep down I knew my demands were futile, but panic had begun to take over any rational thought. "Do you hear me?" I yelled into the tiny port.

Yes, I can hear you, the voice of the room answered back.

"Then make him bring her back!" I screamed at the ceiling.

After pounding the wall with my fist, I began to pace the room. About every ten seconds I glanced up at the digital clock on the wall. The world moved in slow motion.

Fifteen minutes passed. When the clock read 7:00 a.m. my breasts began to tingle, filling for Ella's morning feeding time, but she wasn't there to relieve the pressure. By 7:15 they began to ache.

Finally, I showered and got dressed, more in an effort to distract myself than anything, and then I resumed my pacing. Ella's absence made me feel like a part of me was missing, as if an actual, physical piece of my body had been ripped away.

At 7:45 the door zipped open and Ella's wail of hunger filled the room.

Nurse Gupta held her away from his body, supine on the palms of his hands. His eyes were wide and he clearly had no idea what to do with the howling infant.

In three strides I crossed the room and scooped Ella into my arms.

"Did you take her out of my room this morning?" The

look on my face must have scared him even more because he backed away from me, holding his now empty hands palm out as if to protect himself.

"N-no, Dr. Ammon came to get her. I-I was not even in the room where he had her, he simply called me when he finished and told me to take her back to you."

"Go," I commanded.

Nurse Gupta seemed all too happy to comply. He turned to the keypad and had opened and exited the door in a handful of seconds.

Ella had stopped wailing and was now rooting with her tiny mouth, stretching as far as she could go to get to the milk that she must have been able to smell. I sat on the couch and once she latched on, we both relaxed.

The pressure of too much milk began to wane in a blessedly painful series of long drinks from Ella. She was hungry, and determined. It didn't take long for her to empty both sides and then fall into a peaceful milk-induced sleep.

My head rested on the back of the couch. I held her and closed my eyes, exhausted after a solid forty five minutes of panicking. I must have dozed off as well because when my eyes opened again I could barely lift my head for the crick that had formed in my neck.

No one came the next day, or the next. Sleep eluded me both nights. Every sound, every pause in Ella's breathing, and every imagined shadow on the wall had me bolting upright to make sure no one had taken Ella. I paced and fretted the days away wondering when they were going to come and what I would say.

The lack of sleep and constant worry began to take its toll. I was tired and irritable. Ella kept me going through it all, blissfully oblivious so long as she was full and dry.

Finally, on the third day, the suspense ended. Dr. Ammon entered my room unannounced.

He was lucky that I happened to be changing Ella at the time or I would have strangled him. Unfortunately, the most I could do was glare while I cleaned poo from a baby's bottom. This undoubtedly lacked the intimidation factor I hoped for, but it was the best I could do.

"What do you want?" I could practically feel my lips curling when I spoke.

"Based on the results of the last test, I would like to conduct a trial round of the protein replacement treatment to see how she responds." Dr. Ammon spoke calmly, as if he had never taken my daughter without my permission, as if he hadn't spent the last two days silently torturing me, and now this.

His words hit me like the air bullets I used to stun fish. My fingers stopped moving, my mind seemed to stop working. I stared at Ella without blinking.

"Does she have a developmental disorder?" I asked, though I really didn't want to hear the answer.

"The results are currently inconclusive. Her responses were…unusual."

My teeth clenched and unclenched. Deep inhalations made my nostrils flare. I tried to get myself under control. Her responses were *unusual*, not conclusive. Did he think my daughter was a lab rat?

"What if I refuse the treatment?" I said softly.

"Then you would not be helping Ella, or anyone else. Would you refuse to do what is best for your child?" His calm, his well-rested countenance that lacked the dark circles which bruised the skin beneath my eyes, and his response all made me hate him in that moment.

"What's best for my child is to be with me, not poked and prodded and taken from me without my consent." I hissed the last words through clenched teeth as I struggled to keep my volume in check.

"Yes, I'm sorry about that. It was necessary."

"Do you realize the legal ramifications of all of this? You have a new, no doubt expensive, facility here. I would think you would want to have your patients saying good things about it."

Dr. Ammon paused and narrowed his eyes for the briefest of seconds.

"I'll be back tomorrow morning at 7:30." With that he turned, and left.

"Seven thirty. I am the only patient in this entire damned birthing center and he has to come at seven freaking thirty," I mumbled to myself while I bounced Ella and paced in front of the windows.

I tried to stay mad, or at least frustrated. I hoped it would help me from giving in completely to the fear that threatened to overwhelm me.

CHAPTER 8

Sure enough, at seven-thirty sharp, Dr. Ammon showed up to take us to his lab.

"Where's Nurse Gupta?" I asked.

"He's been reassigned," Dr. Ammon replied.

"Where's Nurse Bell?"

"Still in Portland."

"Wasn't there another patient coming? Who's helping her?"

Dr. Ammon didn't answer this time, just gave me a look and then opened the door to his lab. I stepped through, feeling jittery and anxious.

He nodded toward my usual chair and I sat, but kept shifting, unable to find a comfortable position.

Dr. Ammon attached the now familiar wireless probes to Ella's scalp and turned on his monitors. I stared at the rotating see-through brain, trying to determine if there had been any visible change.

When Dr. Ammon approached again with his syringe

tipped with a small, thin needle, I had to clench my hands and my jaw in an effort to keep myself under control. My breathing became shallow and more rapid the closer the needle got to my daughter.

"This is the protein that will bond with any abnormal cells. The last test showed that she does demonstrate some atypical neural response patterns, but they're not similar to any of the response patterns I've seen in previous patients. I'm hoping that after a few days, I'll be able to look again and see that some of those atypical responses have altered into more typical response patterns. This will let me know that she is a candidate for this type of treatment."

"You don't already know that? I thought that was the point of coming here, because you'd be able to provide treatment if she needed it." I could hear the panic in my voice and tried to push it away, until he brought the needle to Ella's forehead.

"What are you doing? Aren't you supposed to put it in her arm?"

"No, the largest and most prominent vein in an infant is in the head. It's standard procedure for patients this young and will prevent damaging the tiny veins in the arms."

I had to hold my breath and my stomach flip-flopped. I held Ella's tiny hand and watched the needle pierce the vein on Ella's scalp.

"That is just wrong," I whispered.

Ella stirred slightly in her sleep, but didn't wake up, or cry.

Tears formed in my eyes.

"That's my brave girl," I murmured, more for me than for her I suppose.

When he removed the needle, I sighed with relief and began to breathe again.

Dr. Ammon returned to his screens, tapped a few icons, and then dropped several still shots of Ella's brain into a digital folder on one of the monitors.

"Now, talk to her," Dr. Ammon instructed.

"She's asleep," I replied, frowning.

"Her brain will still respond to the sound."

I shrugged and searched for something to say. Everything that came to mind seemed silly, and I didn't want to wake her up. I decided to sing her our lullaby, softly so that Dr. Ammon could barely hear me. Not that he paid attention to me anyway, his eyes were glued to the 3D image of Ella's brain.

When I looked at the monitor after I'd begun singing, I saw areas light up, different areas than I remembered from the last time.

"Is that what happens when she hears my voice?" I asked, fascinated in spite of my fear.

Dr. Ammon nodded but didn't look away. Instead he reached out and touched different parts of the image with a fingertip, causing message boxes to appear in the air around the brain. He tapped a message box and then typed on a keyboard which rested on one of the portable trays.

"Keep singing please."

Startled to realize I'd been watching him in silence, I resumed my song and returned my attention to Ella.

I could hear the clicks of the keyboard as he typed new messages and I wished that I could read the notes. Oddly enough, at the time, I didn't think to ask. I guess I assumed he would tell me if there was anything I needed to know.

Several minutes later my voice began to crack until my dry, tired throat gave out. The song died away and Dr. Ammon didn't tell me to continue. I rested my forehead on the edge of the table where Ella had begun to stir.

"All right, that's it for today. We're going to give her forty-eight hours and then check again to see if there have been any changes."

It took all of my energy to lift my head and stand. I gathered Ella into my arms and shuffled back to my door. I hated that I couldn't just go in, I had to wait for Dr. Ammon to let me in my own room.

Over the next two days Ella grew fussier. She didn't sleep well, which meant I didn't sleep well, and even nursing didn't seem to calm her the way it used to. I felt like a zombie, baggie-eyed, tousled hair and covered in spit-up because every time Ella slept I slept, and every time she woke I needed to feed, change or comfort her. I hadn't been out of this hospital in fourteen days. I think. I had kind of lost track of time. I hadn't spoken to anyone but Dr. Ammon in, what had it been now? At least five days? I wished desperately for Nurse Bell, even Nurse Gupta, or better yet a damn phone signal so that I could call someone that I knew and have them come and pick me up.

I started asking Stella, the disembodied voice of my prison cell, random questions just to hear another voice.

The third morning after Ella's first treatment I managed to take a shower and get dressed while Ella slept. That small act of normalcy felt like a miracle. I tried to look calm and competent when Dr. Ammon came to get us.

"Is Nurse Bell back yet?" I asked, trying to sound casual.

"No, not yet."

As we exited my room I saw Nurse Gupta enter another room down the hall.

"Is there another patient? Could I see her?" I felt a sudden intense need to be around another person, someone other than the taciturn Doctor.

He never responded.

That morning stands out very clearly in my memory now. I recall the image of Ella's brain, the way the lights appeared when I sang, and Dr. Ammon's unwavering attention to the monitors. He seemed…eager. It's like a photograph in my mind that I can bring up in perfect detail and it always sends shivers down my spine.

"Her response patterns have changed slightly, but again, they've changed in a way that I haven't seen before. She's creating new neural pathways beyond what's expected for her age."

"What does that mean?"

Dr. Ammon paused and finally said, "It means I need to do more tests."

Something inside of me snapped.

"No," I replied without hesitation, and with far more conviction than I'd felt about anything for a very long time. "Absolutely not. She's had enough tests. We've been here for too long already. If she needs additional treatment or visits or whatever, we'll do them in Portland, *after* we've gone home. We are going home."

Dr. Ammon turned to me and gave me look that made my heart clench.

"Oh? And how do you plan to get there?" His voice remained calm, his expression neutral, but I felt a wave of fear nonetheless.

"Are you threatening me?" I half stood and felt a flush rise up my neck. "I demand that you take us home. You can't keep us here!" Panic began to creep into my voice because I knew that unless he allowed us to go, he really could keep us here, locked in my room. I couldn't even open the door.

"You are not in a position to be making demands, Miss Wexler." Dr. Ammon's voice seemed to grow colder.

"I refuse to continue. I'll sign whatever I have to sign. I'll talk to Dr. Myers about continuing the treatment with her if Ella needs it, but I am done here. If you continue I swear I will find a way to shut this place down."

This time Dr. Ammon didn't respond. He walked away from me and tapped out his screens, turned off his monitors. He came back and peeled the sensors from Ella's head and finally walked out of the lab, leaving the door open.

I hesitated for a moment, wondering if my demands had worked. My hands shook as I picked Ella up. When I walked out of the examining room I allowed a small sliver of hope to wedge itself into the well of anxiety which had filled my heart ever since we'd arrived here.

Dr. Ammon waited in front of the door to my room. I

held my head high as I approached, but he did not glance at me. He simply waved his hand in front of the scanner and the door opened. I held my breath when I passed him and entered my room.

"Someone will be here in the morning to collect you." I heard him say just before the doors zipped closed.

A long exhale deflated my chest, taking some of the tension from my muscles. A small smile played at the corners of my mouth and tears formed at the corners of my eyes. I felt relieved and I felt powerful.

We were going home.

When was the last time I'd smelled the sea air? Even the overpowering scent of fish guts and seaweed permeating the docks of the sea farm would be a welcome alternative to the stale silence of this room.

Tomorrow. Tomorrow we would finally be on our way!

Excitement kept me going throughout that long day. I packed my bags in preparation. I paced and told Ella all about Cliff Island while I changed her and bounced her and nursed her. I even showered again and shaved my legs while she took a nap.

By bedtime the adrenaline had worn off. I needed sleep. Unfortunately, Ella did not have the same agenda.

She fussed and squirmed and cried no matter what I tried. I checked her diaper every thirty seconds only to find it dry. I tried to feed her, paced, bounced, sang until I went hoarse, but she would not be consoled. So, I did the only thing left to do; I cried with her.

I sat on the couch and held her and we cried until we both fell asleep.

The sound of the door opening made me jerk awake. My startle response woke Ella, who immediately began to cry again.

My eyelids felt gritty and swollen. A crick in my neck made it painful to turn and look toward the doorway. I had to blink several times before I could focus on the figure stepping through the door. Correction, figures.

Dr. Ammon was the first one through. I didn't recognize the other man at first, not until he turned to the side and a flash of memory penetrated the haze of my sleep-deprived brain. The boat driver.

Synapses started firing then.

The boat driver! Is it morning already? Time to go home!

After shifting my body into a sitting position, which is no easy task when both arms are full of sleeping baby, I leaned forward and stood, then read the clock.

It was 4:00 a.m.

A glance out the window revealed that it was still dark, like middle of the night dark. My brow furrowed. It seemed like an odd time to leave.

"I'm all packed. My bags are there, by the door." My voice cracked and had that nasal first-time-I've-spoken-today quality.

"I made an ID card for Ella, just until she's old enough for an implant." Dr. Ammon held up a card and I glanced at it briefly. I held my hand out to take it, but he'd already reached down to grab one of my bags.

The boat driver, Rafael, reached down and took the

other. Without a word they turned and Rafael held a hand in front of the scanner. The door opened and for the briefest of seconds I found myself surprised that he didn't have to enter a code, and then I remembered Nurse Bell explaining that he and Dr. Ammon had the same clearance.

Why on God's green Earth does the boat driver have the same clearance as the lead physician? I wondered. *Head of security also has clearance,* I remembered, *but if he's head of security why is he driving me home?*

Anticipation soon pushed aside all other thoughts. I followed Dr. Ammon down the hallway and toward the exit.

The halls were eerily quiet. We left the spoke and entered the wheel section of the hospital. Not a soul walked the halls save myself and my escorts. Even the reception desk had been abandoned. The rest of the island slept.

I listened to the music of the water falling over the rocks in the corner of the waiting room and marveled at the fact that it had only been about two weeks since I had been through here before. It seemed like a lifetime.

When the rotating door opened to the outside the smell of salt water washed over me like a healing balm. Wind whipped my hair around my face and I curled my body to shield Ella from the light sprinkle falling from the dark clouds above.

Between the needles of rain and the hair blowing in my face, I couldn't watch well where we were going. I kept my head down and followed the feet in front of me until we finally reached shelter and headed down a short flight of stairs toward what I assumed was one of the marinas.

My steps grew more confident as I descended. With one hand I tucked the stray hair back behind my ears. We paused at the base of the stairs. Dr. Ammon waved Rafael through first. The driver scanned his ID, entered a code, and stood motionless while the security system took a retinal scan. Finally, he moved to the side to allow Dr. Ammon space to do the same.

Dr. Ammon then held up the card he'd made for Ella.

"Now you," he said to me and stepped aside.

With a flutter in my chest I held up my hand. After three seconds the light turned green and the door opened.

We walked into the sheltered marina and I heard the sound of waves lapping and splashing. Water washed in and back out again, but never touched the elevated boats. It looked like it might be a rough ride.

I considered saying something, asking if we should wait for the weather to clear, but I feared that if I asked, Dr. Ammon would comply. If we didn't go now, we might never leave, so I hurried down the dock toward the same small boat we'd arrived in.

The driver stepped in first and took the bag that Dr. Ammon held out to him. I waited while Rafael shoved the bags under one of the seats, then Dr. Ammon held out a hand to help me into the boat.

After shifting Ella, I accepted the help, reaching out and gripping his left hand with my right. I began to step into the boat, and then cried out when I felt a sudden sharp pain in my right arm.

My head swiveled to Dr. Ammon, who pressed the plunger of a syringe, forcing fluid into the vein inside the crook of my elbow.

My eyes widened in shock. I tried to step back onto the dock to pull my arm free.

A meaty hand wrapped around my left bicep and then my vision began to blur.

The last thing that I remember was the boat driver taking Ella out of my too-heavy arm before my world went black.

CHAPTER 9

PAIN FINALLY PULLED me out of my chemical-induced sleep. I pried open one eyelid, followed slowly by the other, and saw a white wall which met a white floor maybe an arm's length from the end of my nose.

A thin mattress supported my weight. I pushed up from it with one arm and a wave of nausea forced me back down. I rolled onto my back, then slowly to my other side and scanned a room that looked very similar to my previous bedroom.

There was no sign of Ella.

My breasts, engorged with undrunk milk, ached and had begun to leak.

Two doorways broke up the monotony of the white on white room. One lacked an actual door so I could see the tiny bathroom with its sink, toilet, and shower stall crammed into a space the size of a closet. The other door was closed.

In agonizing increments, I stood and placed one

hand against the wall for support. Hope fought against dread. My heart pounded and my stomach curled itself into knots. Surprisingly, once I was an arm's length from the door, it opened. The suddenness of it made my head jerk backwards, which set the room to spinning. I had to close my eyes and take several long, deep breaths before I could proceed.

A smaller version of my previous living and dining room opened before me. Two significant differences included the lack of a desk and the fact that one full wall and half of the curving ceiling were made of long, clear panels, revealing the fact that my current room was at least half submerged under water.

My steps were tentative at first, fear and uncertainty lurked as I started a slow circuit of the main room. No immediate danger presented itself, so my strides grew longer until my search became frantic. I checked every drawer, every corner, every inch of every room three times. A huge lump of raw emotion lodged itself in my chest, making it hard to breath.

In the middle of my fourth fruitless circuit, I stopped at the main entrance to my suite. My hands slid along the walls, up, over, down the doorframe, desperate to find a scanner, a button, a switch, anything that might provide a glimmer of a chance of getting out of there.

I did find a scanner. No keypad, just a flat, reflective black rectangle to the right of the door. With my heart pounding against my ribs, I held my hand up and waited…and waited. Nothing happened. This didn't surprise me so much as squelch the last flicker of hope which had temporarily burned in my heart.

"Ella," I whispered her name and my hand fell to my side. I pressed my forehead against the door and balled my hands into fists.

"Where's Ella?" I asked, and then I paused and waited for the room to answer.

Silence.

"Ella!" This time I screamed, a scream that threatened to tear my throat. A scream so hard it shattered the thing which had lodged in my chest and I slid to the floor. Sobs wracked my body.

As I whispered Ella's name over and over, a hazy image of the boat driver, Rafael, surfaced in my mind's eye. We were in the boat, he had taken Ella out of my arms.

Where had he taken her? Where had they taken me?

I tried to remember something, anything between that moment and the one when I'd opened my eyes in the white room...nothing.

Was I on another island? A different part of the same island? Where the hell was Ella?

Turning so that my back rested against the wall, I pulled my knees into my chest and pressed against them. I felt milk soak through the front of my shirt and into the thighs of my pants. Wherever she was, she must be hungry. She needed me.

This thought lit a whole different type of fire inside of me.

I turned again and began to pound my fists against the door.

"Can anyone hear me?" I yelled. "I need to see my daughter! Where's my daughter?"

My pounding grew harder the longer I waited with no response. I screamed, then cried, then screamed again as I beat against the door.

Eventually a blood vessel burst in the meat of each hand and the pain forced me to stop pounding. I stared at the purple splotches and watched them expand. I tried to focus on this small, manageable pain so that I wouldn't have to face the much, much bigger one threatening to consume me.

No longer able to beat on the door, I stood and began to pace.

The nausea I'd initially experienced seemed to have been burned away by panic. I was now aware of the eerie silence of the room, the kind of silence that works its way under your skin and makes you want to scream just to hear some noise.

Always before I'd had the sound of Ella's breathing, or Ella's crying. Now the silence surrounded me and pressed in like the weight of the water above.

Hours passed and exhaustion began to fight for my attention, even over the pain of my now inflamed chest and swollen hands.

I lay on the couch, struggling against sleep, afraid of lying unaware. Every time my eyes closed, my mind showed me flashes of horror, like a poorly spliced film reel of the events at the marina. I saw Dr. Ammon stab a needle into my arm and watched Rafael take Ella. I relived hours of screaming and pounding on the door of my room, only to wake up sweating and panting.

Each time I woke reality crashed into me and I would search frantically, pointlessly.

Where is my daughter?

Finally, I curled into a ball on the bed and wept as if sorrow were the only emotion left in the world.

For me, perhaps it was.

CHAPTER 10

No one came to my room that day, or the next. I was forced to order food from the machine on the wall, even though doing something as normal as eating felt completely wrong.

I yelled once for help into the shaft which held the tiny food elevator when it opened for me to retrieve my eggs and salsa. My words were cut off by the warning buzzer, letting me know the door was about to close.

I found no joy in the consumption of my once favorite meal. It eased the ache in my stomach, only to accentuate the ache in my heart.

At the end of the second day I took a shower. I know this seems like an insignificant event, but when you are in the throes of unimaginable grief, finding the will to get out of bed is a small miracle. In truth it was probably the smell that drove me, or the need to rid my skin of the sticky mess which leaking milk had created all over my chest and shrinking abdomen.

By this time, even the water spraying from the showerhead made me wince when it battered my engorged breasts. They were hard and full, like two cantaloupes someone had glued to my ribcage, and they were hot to the touch. One had an angry red streak working its way from the nipple to my heart. It was a constant reminder that my daughter was somewhere without me, not being nourished by my body, not being held by my arms.

After scrubbing thoroughly but gently with soap, I stood under the scalding waterfall with my eyes closed for the last two minutes before the water turned itself off. My bare feet found the red exes on the floor as I stepped out of the shower stall. This activated the forced air dryers in the wall and I stood with my arms outstretched. Beads of water slid across my skin before they evaporated.

My bags had been left in the bedroom, but all of Ella's things had been taken. The knot in my stomach twisted even tighter. My mind filled with the worst scenarios imaginable while I dressed in a clean, dry outfit.

The shower did much to rejuvenate me. I felt determined for a full ten seconds, until I remembered that there was absolutely nothing I could do. I dug through my bag for lack of any other distraction and discovered that my cell phone was gone.

My knees gave out and I sat heavily on the edge of the bed. I didn't cry. I think all of my tears had finally dried up, or I simply lacked the energy to feel anything anymore. I must have stared at the empty pocket where my phone had been for a full ten minutes before I turned my head and let out a long exhale.

My last connection to the world was gone.

There was nothing to do, nothing I could do, so I lay down on the bed and stared at the ceiling until I finally fell asleep.

When I woke, heat burned from my chest all the way up to my forehead and out to the palms of my hands.

A low moan forced its way through my clenched teeth when I tried to sit up. I eased my head back on to the pillow and tried to take shallow breaths. The rise and fall of my ribs sent needles of white hot pain shooting through my breasts.

Eventually, the faint snick of a door opening cut through my fever-induced haze. I remember thinking I should have felt scared, maybe helpless. Instead I felt relieved. *A person, someone who might be able to help, someone who might answer my questions.*

As the person's face came into focus, rage gave me the strength to prop myself on one elbow.

"Where is my daughter?" I forced the words through my raw throat and they came out sounding almost as fierce as I felt.

Dr. Ammon didn't respond.

He stopped at the side of my bed before he reached out and pressed two fingers to the inside of my wrist.

"Where is my daughter?" I repeated yanking my wrist away from his touch.

I flinched when he reached out with his free hand and brushed a strand of hair behind my ear.

"I need to take your temperature," he stated.

My head began to swim, forcing me to lie back against

the pillow. The aural thermometer felt like an icicle pressed against my burning flesh when the tip touched my ear canal.

"Please, is Ella all right?"

"She's fine."

The knot in my gut untwisted ever so slightly. She was safe, she was alive, *if* I could trust what Dr. Ammon told me. I needed to believe those words and besides, what reason did he have to lie to me now?

"What's that?" I asked, trying to slide away from Dr. Ammon. He had uncapped a syringe and dipped the long needle into a fluid-filled vial.

He braced the vial and needle with one hand as he pulled the plunger up, drawing the fluid out of the tube. When the glass tube was empty, he pulled the needle from the vial and moved toward me.

I tried to scramble across the mattress, but I couldn't escape fast enough to prevent one cold hand from gripping my wrist.

"It's an antibiotic," he stated. "You have mastitis."

Blinking hard, I watched the needle enter my vein.

"What's mastitis?"

"An infection in your breast caused by a blocked milk duct."

"It wouldn't be blocked if you'd let me feed my daughter! Where is she? She needs me!" I paused and blinked back the tears which suddenly threatened to spill. I would not cry for this man. "She needs me."

His eyes met mine and my mouth went dry. I saw

no sympathy, no compassion. A shiver worked its way through me. Finally, he released my wrist.

"I'll administer another dose tonight and again tomorrow. You should start to feel better very soon."

I turned my face away from him. The only act of defiance I could muster at that moment.

When I heard the main door close, I curled around a second pillow, buried my face in the rain-scented cover and screamed.

Sleep came in fitful spurts while I waited for Dr. Ammon's return.

He came as promised later that same evening. We did not speak. By morning I felt better, physically. I waited for him on the couch instead of lying in bed and when he drew out his syringe and small clear vial, I held out my arm and looked him in the eye while he administered the antibiotic.

"I'm on the same island, aren't I, just on the lower level." I watched his face, hoping to get my answer from his expression. Much to my surprise, he responded.

"Yes."

At least I knew where I was.

"One more round of antibiotics should be all you need, but you must stop manually expressing the milk. Once you dry up, you'll no longer be susceptible to infection."

"I don't want my milk to dry up, I-" I stopped suddenly when the rest of his message registered. "How do you know that I'm manually expressing milk?"

He raised one eyebrow as he withdrew the needle and nodded for me to hold the cotton ball in place. Once he'd put away his supplies he looked deliberately up and over to the trim along the top of the walls.

My gaze followed, taking in the shiny white strip which ran the full length of the room. It continued along the back wall above the door, reflecting the light in a way that the wall did not. Realization dawned.

"A surveillance strip," I whispered. "You're watching me."

Anger and embarrassment warred caused a flush of heat to spread up my neck.

"Why am I here?"

Dr. Ammon had stood and he held his small kit in his hand, ready to leave. He paused when he heard my question.

"Research," he finally replied.

My breath caught in my throat. He was halfway to the door when I said, "You are continuing the tests on Ella." This was a statement, not a question. I knew without a doubt it was true. Why it hadn't occurred to me before I do not know.

"Yes, I am."

I launched myself off the couch at the same time that he waved his hand in front of the scanner. He was through and closed the door before I could reach him. I slammed my fists against the unyielding surface and screamed my frustration. Then I stopped, and I looked up.

A cold chill crept down my spine and spread, raising goose bumps in its wake. I unclenched my fists and rubbed my arms with opposite hands, my eyes glued to the trim at the junction of wall and ceiling.

Slowly I walked the length of the room and entered the bedroom, only to find the same shiny trim throughout. Much to my horror, it extended into the bathroom.

My face flushed, thinking of Dr. Ammon watching me shower and change. He clearly had watched if he'd seen me trying to relieve the pressure in my breasts with my hands.

As quickly as it had come, my shame burned away, replaced now by a fierce, hot anger. He'd heard me scream for my daughter. He'd watched me pound on the door until my veins burst. He'd seen me cry myself to sleep and he'd done nothing.

What kind of person could do such a thing?

The next day, I learned the extent of what I was up against.

When Dr. Ammon darkened my doorstep and 7:30 a.m., I was ready and waiting. The infection had cleared. The absence of pain had left my mind free to fill with righteous anger. Accusations rested on the tip of my tongue. I swallowed them when the door opened and two men entered.

Dr. Ammon was one of them of course. The other was Rafael.

My fingers curled into white-knuckled fists. My knees bent and my fists rose up in response to a pure fight or flight reaction.

"What is he doing here?" I snapped.

"He's my assistant and I needed his help."

"Well I don't want his help. I don't want to see his face."

"Then feel free to close your eyes." Dr. Ammon stopped a few feet away from me and spoke in his calmest voice. Rafael smirked. I lunged for him.

My curled fingers unfolded and I aimed the nails I hadn't cut since I'd arrived right at his eyeballs.

Dr. Ammon caught one arm and Rafael caught the other.

I struggled for a handful of seconds, but knew it was useless, even if I got away, where would I go?

"Sit down please," Dr. Ammon instructed once I'd stopped thrashing. "At the table," he added, nodding toward the single chair and small round dining table at the opposite end of the kitchen counter.

"Let go of me," I demanded.

"Are you going to sit?"

My nostrils flared. I wanted to defy him, to refuse, to spit in his face. Instead I nodded.

Never turning my back to the two men, I walked backwards with one arm sliding along the counter. I gasped when my elbow hit the glass vase, which held fake flowers and a bottom full of marbles. It wobbled but I managed to grab it in time to prevent it from falling.

Flustered and anxious, I sat coiled like a caged animal in the curved-back chair and watched the men approach.

Dr. Ammon followed and stopped at my right side. He withdrew his small medical kit and placed it on the table. He unzipped the pouch and removed the now familiar syringe and vial. Rafael moved to my left side, too close to my left side.

I shifted away from him in my seat. The hair on the

back of my neck stood up when Rafael placed a hand on my shoulder. I turned and glared at him, then shrugged his hand off as Dr. Ammon gripped my wrist.

"What did you need his help with? You've done this by yourself every day."

Instead of aiming the needle at the vein inside my elbow, Dr. Ammon pointed the sharp tip at the meat of my palm. I began to pull away and felt strong fingers wrap around my upper arms and press them tight to my sides while simultaneously pushing my body down into the seat.

Rafael's hands.

"Hey, what are you doing?" I shrieked. The needle pierced my palm, but I held still, afraid that any movement might jam the needle further into my flesh.

My breath came and went in shallow gasps. My hand began to go numb.

Dr. Ammon kept a firm grip on my wrist as he withdrew and the needle and exchanged the syringe for a tiny but wicked looking scalpel.

"What the-" I tried to pull away then, to wriggle out of Rafael's grasp. I managed to get my body an inch or two off the chair and landed one solid kick to Dr. Ammon's shin.

Rafael immediately turned his body so that one of his heavy legs draped over mine and then shifted his arms so he held my upper body in a tight hug. I could feel his breath tickling my ear and I shuddered.

Fear bubbled from my gut and spread like a virus all the way to my numb fingertips. The logical part of my brain knew that I couldn't get free, knew that I had nowhere to hide, but my instincts were not interested in logic.

My muscles strained against Rafael's weight, which forced him to tighten his hold and draw closer to me.

Dr. Ammon pressed the back of my hand down on the table, scalpel poised to make its first cut.

Beads of sweat stood out on my forehead and the back of my neck. I watched the honed edge bite into the flesh of my palm.

"What the hell are you doing?" I screeched. My body tensed in preparation for the flash of pain that did not come.

One shallow cut was all he made before he set down the scalpel and pulled out a hair thin wire.

Dr. Ammon pressed down with his thumb just in front of the cut he'd made, which revealed a small slit in my palm. He pushed the wire into the slit with expert precision.

As he pulled the wire slowly back out, a tiny chip came out with it, affixed to the end of the wire.

My ID.

"What are you doing? What are you going to do with that?" My voice had become breathy with disbelief and, I'm ashamed to say, quite desperate.

Dr. Ammon placed the chip in the tiny case he'd laid open on the table and held it down with one finger as he removed the wire and placed a lid on the case. He continued to ignore me. I watched him set the wire down beside the case and clean the cut. Finally, he withdrew a tube from his bag, uncapped it, and squeezed. A thin line of clear adhesive covered the incision site.

Rafael removed his leg and, as he shifted his weight, I lunged for the case which held my ID.

Rafael immediately pulled me back against the chair. Dr. Ammon calmly wiped down his tools, repacked his kit, and then picked up the clear case. He gazed at the tiny chip inside, the chip that could access all of my accounts, my contacts.

"Why are you doing this?"

Dr. Ammon leaned in close, close enough that I could smell the coffee on his breath.

"You and your daughter may very well be the next step in human evolution."

I frowned in confusion, trying to make sense of what he'd said. Meanwhile, he backed away and then turned toward the door. Rafael finally let go of my arms, dragging the fingertips of his left hand across the top of my chest in a way that made my stomach churn.

Without thinking I snapped my head forward and bit the tip of his thumb.

"Son of a-"

"Rafael, let's go."

Rafael glared down at me as he backed away, holding his thumb. I glared back, wishing for my gutting knife.

Finally, the door closed behind them and I began to shake. I wrapped my arms around myself in an attempt to stop the uncontrollable shivers. After a few minutes they subsided and I held my right hand out in front of me, turned it palm up, and uncurled my fingers. I stared at the thin red line. Cold snakes of anxiety writhed in my stomach.

I was an illegal.

No ID, no history, no lines of credit…no daughter.

I could no longer access my e-mail. I couldn't even open most doors on or off this God-forsaken island. Not that I'd ever need to worry about that. My chances of ever leaving this room did not look good.

Several hours passed before I had calmed down enough to eat. Sleep was out of the question.

For two days I didn't shower or change my clothes, too creeped out by the knowledge that someone watched me. I began to look as strung out as I felt.

Finally, the fourth morning after Dr. Ammon and Rafael's visit, I couldn't take it anymore. They'd already seen me naked, what difference did it make?

All the difference in the world.

My skin actually felt like it crawled over my bones as I scrubbed down and waited for the rain-scented water to rinse away the suds. People always used that expression, about skin crawling. I'd understood the meaning, of course, but I'd never fully comprehended the sensation until that moment.

In an effort to speed up the process and get myself clothed once again, I sluiced soap off my skin while the water sprinkled from one of those annoying low-flow shower heads.

As I stepped out of the stall and activated the dryers, I couldn't resist the urge to cover my chest with crossed arms. I didn't dry as thoroughly, but at least I felt less exposed, less vulnerable.

I stepped into a pair of underwear that I'd washed in the bathroom sink and hung to dry, and then pulled on a nursing tank top. I had to adjust the straps and was surprised to see how the shirt draped over my diminishing torso. The sad reminder that the life I'd nourished for so long had been torn from me poured salt in my ravaged heart.

Tears blurred my vision. I tried to blink them away as I finished dressing, but they were persistent. I sniffed and walked out of the bathroom, then through the bedroom. My hands reached up to wipe my cheeks and I closed my eyes for a split second. I stepped into the living room and collided with a very solid object that shouldn't be there.

Startled, I gasped and stepped back.

When I looked up, I saw Rafael.

My heart lodged in my throat. I tried to back away, only to find myself pressed against the living room wall.

"What are you doing here?"

He didn't answer, but his eyes traveled the length of my body, forcing me to fight down a sudden urge to vomit.

When he stepped toward me, I cast my eyes around the room in a desperate attempt to find some sort of weapon. Maybe a knife from one of the drawers? Could I make it there?

I stepped and he reached, catching me by one arm and then he leaned forward, inhaling deeply.

He was smelling my hair. Fear seemed to paralyze my body. I could not move.

"Not a lot of women on this island," he said. "A man gets lonely."

Turning my head, I looked at his face. The face of the man who took my Ella out of my arms.

My body tensed. I coiled my strength, then released it in a single explosive upward thrust that drove the top of my head straight into Rafael's face. I heard a sickening crack and then felt warm wet rivulets run across my scalp.

Rafael released my arm and stepped back, bellowing and covering his nose with both hands.

I ran, belatedly remembering that I had nowhere to hide, but at least I could put distance between myself and my attacker.

Half crouched behind the dining table, I watched him turn to face me, his eyes filled with hatred.

With one sleeve he wiped the blood which still oozed from his nose, leaving a red smear across his upper lip and out onto one cheek.

He approached me warily now. I'd lost the element of surprise.

With a quick side-step, I gripped the sides of the dining room chair and lifted it in front of me as I backed around the table. The legs pointed toward Rafael and I feinted once or twice in an attempt to maintain the distance between us.

He pressed forward and I tried to take a swing at him, but the weight of the chair made my movements slow and awkward. Rafael grasped the front legs and yanked the chair from my hands. I continued to back away as he hurled the chair across the room. I flinched when it bounced off the clear wall which held back several tons of water before it clanged against the smooth white floor.

In the brief second that my eyes followed the chair, Rafael darted forward. He moved so fast I never had a chance to react.

His hands slid down my arms and locked on my wrists. One of his legs swept my feet out from under me, and he twisted me around so that I faced the floor. I fell in slow motion, controlled by his grip on my wrists.

Before I hit the floor, I turned my head to the side so that my right cheek pressed against ground. I felt him shift his grip so that one hand secured both of my wrists while his other hand worked its way under the waistband of my pants. When he lifted the knee that he'd been using to pin my legs to the floor, I rocked my hips and twisted to face him. This pulled him off balance. His weight shifted unexpectedly and his left hand became pinned beneath me.

Before he could recover, I brought one knee up into his ribcage. He grunted but didn't stop in his attempt to keep me subdued.

I tried to roll as he pinned my legs with his knee again, but the arm that I'd trapped beneath me blocked me on one side, his body blocked the other. Rafael jerked his left hand free and then pressed his left forearm across my shoulders and upper chest. He bared his teeth as he once again worked his right hand down my pants.

My insides seemed to turn to water as he began to slide my pants down over my hips. At one point, in order to keep my chest pinned while he tried to get the back of my pants to slide over my butt, which I had pressed against the floor with all my strength, he leaned down and tipped the side of his head toward me. His eyes remained fixed on his task.

Without thinking, I lifted my head, stretching my neck as far as it would go and opened my mouth until my teeth surrounded his earlobe, then I bit down, hard.

Rafael howled and instinctively tried to pull away. I bit down harder. He rose, screaming and clutching his ear. I felt the small lobe on my tongue.

I spit out the bloody piece of flesh and tried not to gag as I scrambled backwards.

Rafael pressed his hand to the side of his head, blood oozed through his fingers.

I stood and grabbed the second dining room chair then swung it with all my might at his kneeling form.

Rafael lifted one arm to block the blow, but didn't lift it high enough. One leg connected with his forearm, the other leg, caught the side of his head.

When he saw me prepare to swing again, he backed away from my second assault but found his retreat blocked by the kitchen counter.

His fingers walked across the countertop and closed around the decorative glass vase. Before I could hit him again, he hurled his weapon. I ducked behind the chair and felt the impact seconds before I heard the glass hit the floor and shatter.

Keeping the chair high, I rushed him and felt the legs of the chair connect. He grunted again, and then I felt the chair slipping from my hands. As he pulled, his blood-slick fingers slid across the smooth metal and he stumbled backwards.

Capitalizing on my momentary advantage, I swung the chair again and this time connected with his already broken nose.

Rafael went to his knees with a roar of pain. I brought the edge of the chair down hard against the back of his head.

He fell forward and hit the floor. The room was suddenly silent.

I hit him again, just to make sure, and then backed away. The chair fell from my shaking hands and clattered against the floor. I pressed a hand against my heaving chest.

Blood pounded through my veins, causing the cut in my hand to throb with remembered pain.

My hand. My ID.

My eyes shifted to Rafael and I stared for several seconds at his inert form. My gaze traveled from his ripped ear down his blood-soaked shirt to his right hand.

He could open my door.

Warily, I approached him. Scenes of countless people in countless movies who walked over to the fallen monster while the audience screamed at them to run played through my head. That was me now. I could hear my mind screaming at me to run, but there was nowhere to go.

Rafael would wake up eventually, or Dr. Ammon would come. Maybe he was on his way now.

I knelt down slowly, my whole body tense and ready to spring at the first sign of movement. Staring at his hand I wondered what to do. Should I drag him to the door? Even if I managed to get him to the door and then lift him high enough to reach the scanner, I'd never get out of the building, or off the island. I had to take his ID with me.

I'd watched Dr. Ammon take mine, but he'd had the appropriate tools. I had nothing. Then I remembered the vase.

Creeping across the floor, I tried to remain silent, afraid I might alert my unconscious assailant to my intentions.

After retrieving a large piece of glass with a particularly sharp point, I returned to my victim. I prodded him with the toe of my shoe. His ribs lifted slightly when I pushed, but when I stepped back he flopped bonelessly back into place and remained still.

My heart pounded so hard I could hear it in the too-silent room. My palms grew slick and I was forced to rub them across my thighs before I could begin. My fingers shook. I reached down and gripped Rafael's right hand and flipped it palm up.

I watched his face and took a deep breath, then exhaled as I lowered the piece of glass toward the faint white scar which marked the original incision point of his chip implant. The sharp point of the glass pressed into his flesh. I winced but forced myself to press down harder and drag it across the meat of his palm.

A line of vivid red bloomed in the wake of the glass.

I tried to imagine that his pale palm was the belly of a fish, that this was just another day at the docks.

Rafael moaned slightly and his hand twitched in the way that people do when they're having a bad dream.

"Welcome to my world," I whispered, swallowing down the nausea that threatened to undo me.

I held my breath and turned the glass to make a small cut down toward his wrist. I then inserted the tip of the glass into the opening I'd made and lifted the small flap of skin. I said a quick prayer of thanks for my lack of nail clippers during my incarceration. I used the points of my fingernails to retrieve the tiny clear shield that held Rafael's ID chip inside.

Rafael moaned again and this time shifted his head. His eyes remained closed but I dropped his hand and scuttled backwards until I ran into the wall. I held his ID in my fingertips.

Please let this work. Please let this work. Standing on rubbery legs, I repeated this mantra and walked toward the door.

My head began to pound when I held the chip in front of the scanner to the right of my door.

Nothing happened.

"Come on," I whispered. My hand dropped to my side and I turned when I heard a moan and a scuffle behind me.

Rafael was waking up.

His head lifted and my stomach plummeted to the bottom of my gut when his eyes met mine.

Turning back to the scanner, I lifted the chip again

and held it steady for several seconds. My heart quailed when I heard Rafael pull himself to his feet. I forced myself not to look back.

A half-sob of relief escaped my throat when the door opened.

I stepped through before it had fully recessed in the wall and turned to hold the chip in front of the scanner on the other side of the door.

My knees nearly gave out when I saw Rafael lunge for the opening, a minute too late.

The door to my personal hell closed, with Rafael on the other side.

Dropping my hand, I stepped away, keeping my eyes fixed on that door.

I prayed I would never see that room, or that man, again.

Now, time to find Ella.

CHAPTER 11

THE PROBLEM WAS, I had no idea where to go.

I quick-walked along the curving hallway, occasionally breaking into a jog before slowing again. My sense of urgency battled with practicality. I couldn't decide if I should hurry or try to appear nonchalant in case anyone saw me. My eyes darted from side to side, searching the walls for some kind of sign, a map, or better yet, an elevator.

I was under the water, or at least a part of my room had been. I knew I needed to go up…but how? Where?

The hallway formed one constant curve as it circled the island. Adrenaline coursed through my body while I walked. I moved forward but kept glancing back.

Once when I glanced back, paranoid that Rafael had somehow been able to get out and now pursued me, or that Dr. Ammon had watched the whole encounter and would find me and lock me back in that room, a huff of air was forced from my lungs as I collided with something solid.

I gasped the air back into my body. I looked, even as I prepared to flee, and then stopped.

"Nurse Bell!" The name came out in an explosion of relief.

"Lana?" Nurse Bell's eyes widened until a white ring became visible all the way around both golden brown irises. Her face paled and then flushed, all in a matter of seconds. "Lana, is that really you? I thought you were dead," she whispered.

My brow furrowed and I replied, "Not quite."

"What happened to you?" Nurse Bell had recovered slightly from her initial shock and now scanned me from head to toe.

I looked down at the smears on my pant legs, my torn shirt. I'm sure my hair was a tangled mess.

"It's a long story. First I need to find Ella."

"You need to find...oh!" Nurse Bell covered her mouth with both hands. Tears sprang to her eyes. "Oh my gosh, that was Ella."

"What was Ella? Where is she?" I stepped forward and griped Nurse Bell's forearms. "Is she okay?"

"Yes, she's okay. I just can't believe this. How did this happen? What happened?"

"I'll explain later. Right now I need your help. Will you help me?"

She paused for a moment, looking at me like a deer in the headlights. Finally her expression hardened into something tougher than I'd ever expected to see on the face of Lacy Bell. She nodded once.

"Okay, I need you to take me to Ella."

The look of determination crumbled and her eyes began to glisten again.

"I can't."

My fingers dug into her arms until she winced.

"What do you mean you can't?" I hissed. "You just said you'd help me! I need to see my daughter!"

Nurse Bell tugged her arms until I finally released them. She sniffed and then answered.

"I will help you. I'll do whatever I can, but I can't take you to Ella because Ella is not here."

Her words drove into my heart like a knife.

"Where is she?" I whispered.

"I don't-"

"Where is she?" This time I screamed and Nurse Bell reached out and took my hands.

"Dr. Ammon left this morning with a woman and her child. Remember the one I'd said was waiting to have her baby? She had it while I was on leave. When I came back she had a little girl that I could have sworn was Ella, but Dr. Ammon told me you had both died in a storm on your way back home."

"He gave my baby to another woman?"

"I think so. It has to be Ella. Crap, I was so stupid." Nurse Bell placed a hand over her flat abdomen and then looked down before she closed her eyes and sighed. "I trusted him."

My eyebrows lifted.

"Are you pregnant?" I asked. The only women I'd ever seen who placed a hand on their belly that way knew there was a child just inches away.

Lacy Bell made a sound that was half-laugh, half-sob and nodded.

"And it's because of him," she choked out the words, and then wiped a tear from her cheek.

"You mean it's Dr. Ammon's?" My eyes widened in shock. I didn't know what else to say.

"No, no, it's not what you think. My husband and I found out that we couldn't have kids, went through the whole testing and in-vitro process with no luck. Finally, we met Dr. Ammon and he was the one who told us the specific problem. I could have a child, at least all the tests looked good, my husband couldn't. So, he helped us find a donor that would be a good…uh, fertile…match."

"Oh, got it," I replied holding up a hand. I felt too full of the day's events to really be astonished by more unexpected news, but I was unsure about what Nurse Bell wanted to hear. "You said he's gone?"

Nurse Bell nodded.

My shoulders sagged with relief. Not because he'd left with my daughter, but because he wasn't following me. He hadn't seen what had happened in my room, so he also wouldn't be on his way to free Rafael.

"Well, his *assistant* is also indisposed at the moment. Can we find out where Dr. Ammon went?"

"He said he was taking the patient home, which I thought was kind of strange since he doesn't usually escort patients. I guess the first place we could check is his house on the mainland."

Nurse Bell turned on her heel and tugged on my hand.

"Come on," she said and then led me down the hall. She stopped after we'd passed three more doors and held her hand in front of the scanner outside.

"What's this?" I asked, apprehensive about entering another of these underwater cells.

"My room," Nurse Bell replied. "We need to clean you up before anyone sees you."

After the door opened, I followed Nurse Bell into a room much like the one I'd just left, but with far more personality. There were real flowers in the vase on her kitchen counter and a fleece blanket hanging from the back of her couch which boasted bright contrasting stripes. The floor was covered in several places by expensive-looking rugs.

As I took in hints of the real Nurse Bell, my stomach growled so loud that Lacy laughed.

"How about some breakfast first?"

I sighed but nodded. The thought of sitting and eating, of taking the time to shower and change while my baby got farther away, made me fidget with restless anxiety. Yet I had no choice. I needed energy to continue, and I needed Nurse Bell's help.

The distinctive pop of a refrigerator door opening startled me. I stared in awe. Nurse Bell pulled out fresh vegetables, a bowl of diced fruit, and arranged it all beautifully on two plates.

"You have your own food." I half expected a response

of, "*thank you, Captain Obvious*" but Nurse Bell only smiled and nodded.

She placed both plates on a table identical to my previous one. I slid into the curved-back chair and couldn't help but think of Rafael. The memory made me shudder.

"Tell me what happened," Nurse Bell commanded before placing a forkful of fruit into her mouth.

So, I told her. In between my own mouthfuls of food, I related everything from the day the new nurse had stepped through my door up to the moment I ran into her in the hallway.

About halfway through my story, Nurse Bell stopped eating and stared at me with her eyebrows pulled together, forming a small crease in her otherwise unlined face.

"I don't understand," she admitted after several moments of silence. "Why would he take her from you in the first place, and why would he keep you here?"

I took my last bite of blueberries and spinach, and then I shrugged. Once I'd chewed and swallowed I answered, "I don't know. In between knocking me out and stealing my daughter, he never stopped to explain why."

Nurse Bell seemed to think about this for a moment, and then resumed eating. She chewed slowly and stared out at the water held back only by a thin piece of clear material.

"Is that the ocean?" I asked.

"No, the freshwater lagoon in the center of the island expands under the surface to create ballast, and it holds enough water for normal daily usage."

"I guess that explains why I never saw any fish."

Once the plates were both empty, Nurse Bell took them and washed them in her kitchen sink. She dried them and put them away. I sat there feeling useless.

"Okay," she said, clapping her hands together one time to emphasize her words. "It's time to get you cleaned up and figure out a way to get you out of here."

Nurse Bell waved for me to follow her into her room. The bedroom was the same size mine had been, but a large painting hung on the wall, a picture rested on the nightstand, and clothes were everywhere.

She stepped carefully over one pile at the end of her bed and opened her closet. The hanger bar bowed slightly in the middle under the weight of Nurse Bell's wardrobe.

For several minutes the only sounds in the room were the sandpaper scrape of hangers along the top of the carbon-fiber bar, punctuated by an occasional muffled thump as Nurse Bell tossed an item onto the bed.

"All right, why don't you shower and then try on a few of these to see what fits. Wear something you would feel comfortable swimming in, because I have a feeling you're going to have to get wet."

I raised an eyebrow at her.

"I'll explain when you're done. I've got to look a few things up, check some maps of the island, and make a plan. Towels are in the top drawer under the sink in the bathroom."

"Towels?" I said, surprised that she would have something other than what seemed to be the standard forced-air dryers.

"I brought my own," she explained.

I nodded, but after Nurse Bell left the bedroom, I wrapped my arms around myself and looked up at the ceiling or, to be more precise, the trim at the junction of wall and ceiling. With a sigh of relief I noted the absence of the reflective strip that had been present in my previous quarters.

Confident in the knowledge that no one watched me, that no one *could* watch me, I stripped off my torn and blood-stained clothing and turned on the water in the shower.

For the second time that morning, I reveled in the sensation of hot water sliding across my skin. I felt a little guilty about my water use, but not guilty enough to forgo a good scrubbing.

Once the shower turned itself off, I stepped out and stood dripping on the porous floor for a full minute, waiting for the dryers to turn on, before I remembered that there were towels. Goose bumps stood out on my arms and legs. I shivered as I padded over to the drawer, opened it, and pulled out a mint green towel.

The material felt plush, thick and soft between my fingers, and comforting. I scrubbed down and then wrapped it around my torso.

A part of me dreaded trying on any of Nurse Bell's clothing. She was one of those petite perky people who could probably still shop in the juniors section. At five foot seven I wasn't exactly a giant, but at one month postpartum no one would describe my figure as petite either.

Better tight than blood-stained, I decided.

With a sigh, I began to dig through the pile until I

found a skirt with an elastic waistband and a peasant-style shirt that looked like it had some extra room. They fit well enough, so I saved that for my "after" outfit.

For whatever it was that Nurse Bell had in mind, I pulled on a pair of leggings that were a cotton-spandex blend and a long-bodied t-shirt. Over the t-shirt, which stretched across my chest and stomach, I pulled on a zip front hoodie that was too short in the arms but worked to cover the rest.

When I returned to the living room, I saw Nurse Bell leaning toward the screen which hovered over her desktop, tracing a pattern on the screen with one fingertip.

She glanced up when I stopped a few feet away from where she worked and nodded at my outfit before turning back to the screen.

"So, this is what we're going to do…"

CHAPTER 12

WE STUDIED THE maps together. She explained the layout of the island and determined our rendezvous point.

"Dr. Ammon is gone and Rafael is...contained," she paused and gave me conspiratorial wink. "So, no one else knows who you are or anything about what happened. Act like you belong here, stay calm, and if anyone asks, you're my sister, got it?"

I nodded.

"Why can't we just leave from one of the marinas?" I asked.

"Because security in the marina is tighter. Your eye scan won't match your ID, and neither of us knows Rafael's passcode."

"Oh, right." Nurse Bell had sliced my palm and inserted Rafael's ID into the tiny sleeve where my own should have been. We had to look casual, which meant I needed to be able to hold my palm up to the scanners at the checkpoints.

"Okay, are you ready?"

I nodded and Nurse Bell shut down her computer, grabbed a small bag of belongings and headed for the door.

"My bags," I said, suddenly realizing when I saw her tote that I'd be leaving all of my belongings in the room with Rafael.

"Nothing we can do about that now. I'll have to pick them up some other time."

Again, I nodded. It was just a bag of clothes. Dr. Ammon and Rafael had already confiscated anything that really mattered.

"Coming?" Nurse Bell asked pausing in the open doorway.

"Yep, coming."

Nurse Bell led me around the corner to an elevator, which we took to the main level.

When we stepped outside, I had to stop and shield my eyes. I blinked back the tears which sprung up in response to the first direct natural light I'd been exposed to in weeks.

"You all right?" Nurse Bell asked.

I nodded and sniffed back the mucus which began to fill my nostrils. Sniffing drew the salt air into my nose. The scent of the ocean filled me like a healing balm, filtering through the cracks in my soul and scouring the festering wounds.

"I'm going to get my boat. You know where to meet me?"

When I could finally open my eyes and look around without tearing up, I scanned the surface of the island

and located the narrow point between the two rising walls of the greenhouse and housing complex. I nodded toward the rendezvous point and Nurse Bell nodded in response before heading toward the marina where her boat was stored.

My footsteps fell without a sound on the bright white pathway. I forced myself to control my pace and keep my eyes forward. It felt surreal to see other people casually strolling in the open air. A gardener was visible through the glass of the greenhouse. Several people played mini-golf on the perfect green lawn in the distance. Everything seemed so…normal.

How could such a terrible thing happen in such a beautiful place? I wondered, curling my fingers into a fist in an attempt to hide the cut across my palm.

When I reached the fence which spanned the lowest point on the island, I stopped and stared at the choppy waves below. I didn't see Nurse Bell and her boat yet. I couldn't help but glance around to see if anyone watched.

Adrenaline coursed through my veins and my heart pounded. I feared I might not be able to go through with Nurse Bell's plan, at least until I heard the whir of a hydro-engine and saw Nurse Bell waving as she approached the wall of the Ecopolis.

My mind flooded with memories of Ella and my misgivings disappeared. Inwardly I cringed at the thought of climbing the fence, having only recently healed from my episiotomy, but I had no choice. Ella had a several hour head start. There was no time to waste.

As Nurse Bell cut the engine and waved again, I swallowed my doubts and pulled myself up the chest-high stakes and managed to get one foot up and firmly on the top railing. My arms screamed in protest and I pushed my body weight up to side-plank position, holding it there for at least ten seconds while I worked to get my bottom leg up and over.

There was no way I would be able to get to a standing position. I didn't have the strength to hold on, let alone push up and balance.

This point of the island stood ten feet above sea level. The fence stood another four feet at least. It wasn't a ridiculously dangerous distance, but it would still hurt like hell to belly-flop from that height.

My arms began to shake. I knew I was about to fall. With one last burst of strength, I pushed my whole body forward, pointed my feet toward the waves, and tried to straighten out so I would enter the water feet first.

As I closed my eyes, an image of circling sharks popped unbidden into my mind's eye. I gasped in my final breath and squeezed my eyes shut before icy water enveloped my body.

The moment I was able to move my limbs, I separated my legs and spread my arms to slow my downward movement. I kicked and pushed toward the surface, breathing a prayer of thanks that I'd actually learned to swim.

My head finally broke the surface, allowing me to inhale. Next I pressed the water out of my eye sockets and parted my lids, scanning for Nurse Bell and her boat.

"Come on, the alarm's triggered!"

I looked toward the sound of her voice and found

her leaning over the edge of her small craft about eight feet away.

My body had already begun to go numb from the cold. It took all my willpower to uncurl and stretch my limbs out, exposing all parts to the frigid water. I forced myself to swim toward her outstretched hand.

"Come on!"

My teeth chattered. I kicked toward Nurse Bell and the safety of her boat. Her warm fingers wrapped around my numb wrist. I could barely bend my fingers in response. She pulled and I kicked until I could hook my left arm over the edge of the boat and help haul myself in.

I flopped ungracefully onto the hard bottom of the boat and lay there, thankful to be out of the water and out of the wind. I curled into a ball and willed my skin to soak up some of the sun's warmth. Nurse Bell sped away from my temporary prison.

"There's a towel and some dry clothes in the bow," Nurse Bell called over the hum of the engine. The wind tried to capture her voice and pull it away from my ears. I did manage to hear her, though it was faint.

I nodded in response but made no effort to move until I began to shiver. Desperate then for more warmth, I rolled onto my hands and knees and carefully turned until I faced the bow.

Bluish fingers extended from my pale hand and clutched the towel, then pulled it toward my shivering body. Sitting up with my knees tight to my chest, I wrapped the fluffy terry-cloth around my shoulders and legs and huddled inside, thankful for the warmth.

"How long to the Portland harbor?" I yelled.

"We're not going to the harbor," Nurse Bell called back.

"What?!? I thought we were going to find Ella! We're supposed to find Ella!"

"I know, I know, we will!" The fact that she had to shout prevented Nurse Bell's words from sounding very reassuring. "You won't get past security in the harbor. We've got to go to a private dock."

"Whose private dock?"

Nurse Bell smiled.

"Mine."

CHAPTER 13

ONCE I'D STOPPED shaking, I stripped down, toweled off, and changed into the dry clothes I'd selected from Nurse Bell's wardrobe. I wished now that I hadn't chosen a skirt. The wind lifted and tugged at the hem until I finally tucked the whole thing tight under my legs and laid the wet towel on top.

"How long until we get to your house?" I asked.

"About an hour."

I tried not to let my disappointment show. An hour wasn't so bad, considering, yet I couldn't help but feel that every minute we took was a minute that Ella might be getting farther away.

"How did he get her past security?" I wondered aloud.

Nurse Bell apparently realized which "he" I referred to and barely hesitated before answering.

"I'm sure he made her a fake ID. Hers doesn't have to be implanted yet."

I nodded.

"So, could we still track it?"

"Theoretically, yes, if we went to the police, told them the story, and they believed us. It doesn't help that you have a fake ID, unless they found Rafael and questioned him, or if we could find the woman who left with Ella. She'd be able to verify part of the story at least."

"Can you find her? Find out where she lives?"

"I don't know her name."

"Can't you look up her file or something?"

"She wasn't my patient so I don't have access to her file. I could have checked the registration list, but I didn't think of that before we left. When we get to my house, I'll call the desk, if Brian's working, he might forward me the list."

"And what if he's not?"

"I have a few connections." Nurse Bell paused and then added, "We'll find her, I promise."

Wind caught my hair and pulled it in crazy directions, causing strands to snap back and strike my face like tiny whips, leaving behind lines of itchy memory. I closed my eyes and let the blows fall, trying to keep my focus on the hum of the motor. Vibrations traveled through the floor of the boat and up my legs. Eventually it lulled me to sleep.

A bump rocked me sideways waking me from my nap. The subsequent screech of metal on metal made me cringe and I looked up to see a rocky coastline graduate into lush green lawns.

"Here we are," Nurse Bell announced. I stared and tried to figure out where *here* was.

After a fruitless attempt to smooth the tangled mess that was my hair, I gathered my wet clothes into the towel which Nurse Bell had provided and waited while she secured the boat. She tied on to a white dock which led to a long series of white stairs. The staircase ended at the base of a perfectly manicured lawn complete with the diamond pattern that was the mark of expertly mown grass. The house beyond the lawn was modest in size, for a coastal home, but still elegant by my standards with all its modern angles and huge windows.

Nurse Bell helped me onto the dock and then led the way forward and upward.

When we reached the entrance, Nurse Bell tapped out a series of numbers on a clear panel to the right of the wide, clear double doors. The seal released with a pop and Nurse Bell gripped one of the silver handles and pulled one door open. She gestured for me to step through.

After one tentative step over the threshold, I stopped. Every surface of the house gleamed in the light of the mid-day summer sun.

"Wow," I breathed, taking a step to the side to make room for Nurse Bell. I tried to shift my weight, feeling guilty about leaving even the impression of footprints from the warm soles of my feet meeting the cool floor.

"I know, it's nice isn't it? Too bad no one's ever here to enjoy it." Nurse Bell didn't seem to share my reservations about messing the place up. She tromped right through with her dirty shoes, leaving a visible trail of sand behind her, and then dumped her bag unceremoniously in the middle of the dining room table.

"Are you hungry?" she asked, heading for the fridge. "I am. I can't seem to get enough to eat lately."

A bittersweet smile tugged at the corners of my mouth as I remembered those early months of my pregnancy. I'd been terrified and amazed...mostly terrified.

"I'm fine," I replied. Nurse Bell's head and shoulders disappeared behind the stainless steel door of the fridge.

She reemerged moments later with an armload of packaged food.

"Not as good as the stuff on the island, but it'll fill you up. You sure you don't want anything?"

"I'm sure," I replied and walked to one of the full-length windows. Grey rocks descended into the steel blue water.

The familiar and yet somehow foreign landscape brought on a rush of homesickness like I'd never experienced before. The white masts of a hundred boats speared the blue sky like miniature bolts of lightning through a dark cloud. I recalled at least a hundred days, staring at the choppy waves from my station on the docks, wishing desperately for a different view, a different life. Now I'd give anything to have that back. The simple existence, the predictable schedule, I would never take it for granted again.

Well, almost anything, I corrected. I'd learned hard and fast the one thing I could not live without. I fought back tears as Nurse Bell tore open a package of crackers and munched while she prepared a plate of food.

"Where are we?" I asked, turning and joining her at the table once she sat down.

"We're in Mussel Cove," she replied around a mouthful of fruit.

"Mussel Cove," I repeated, trying to picture a map of the Maine coastline in my head.

"It's about an hour north of Portland. I figured we'd stop here, make a few phone calls, get any supplies we might need, and then head to the city by car so that we could avoid all the checkpoints in the primary harbors."

I nodded, not feeling like I had much choice in the matter.

"You know, I still have your contact list if there's anyone you want to call."

I perked up a bit at that thought, until I considered what I would say, and what my friends would ask.

"I'd better wait until I find Ella," I decided. I wanted desperately to talk to someone, but I needed to maintain my armor. I had to stay strong and keep going until I found my daughter. I feared that the moment I heard a familiar voice I'd break down and not be able to keep going.

"You sure?"

No.

"I'm sure," I said aloud.

"All right then." Nurse Bell scarfed the contents of her plate and placed her dirty dishes in the sink. "Give me fifteen minutes then we can be on our way."

Nurse Bell disappeared down the hallway and I waited.

"Okay." I jumped at the sound of Nurse Bell's voice several minutes later, I'd been so lost in my thoughts I hadn't even heard her approach. "I got a hold of Dr. Myers and she told me to bring you in right away so, let's get out of here."

"Why are we going to see Dr. Myers now?" I asked. "Can she help us find Ella?"

"I don't know, but she can verify your identity and help you get a new implant."

"Oh," I said, looking down at the angry red line across my palm. "I'd kind of forgotten about that."

Nurse Bell grabbed a handful of crackers for the road and led me to her spotless two car garage which currently only housed one small electric car. She noticed my glance at the second, empty space.

"Phil, my husband, is at work."

"Where does he work?" I asked.

"He's a partner on the managerial board of a medical research company."

"Oh, so, what does he do?"

Nurse Bell chuckled and gave me a wry grin.

"Well, mostly he plays golf with other members of the managerial board and discusses business proposals. He's one of the financial advisors so he signs off when funds are drawn from one place and spent in another. Ironically, his company paid for most of Dr. Ammon's research and introduced him to the private backer whose money built the island and the research hospital."

And the web just keeps on tangling, I thought.

"I see," I replied, climbing into the passenger side of the economy car.

Nurse Bell punched a button to open the garage door once I'd closed mine, and the little car zipped out of the enclosure and down the slanted driveway. I gripped the edges of the seat in a white-knuckled grasp. Nurse Bell flew along the curvy coastal road like a driver on Nascar.

Thankfully, traffic forced her to a crawl forty minutes outside the city.

Nurse Bell began to honk her pathetic little horn and I rolled my eyes.

"You do realize that's not going to make anyone move any faster, right?"

Nurse Bell smiled her even-toothed smile and replied, "I know, but it makes me feel better."

I had to smile back.

Eventually, even I wanted to lay on the horn. We inched along at barely a snail's pace.

"How can there be this much traffic in the middle of the day?" I asked.

"It's always like this," Nurse Bell replied, shaking her head. "The city is working to ban vehicles within the city proper, force everyone to use public transportation, but there's no space to put commuter lots. Now they're trying to build parking garages for boats."

"That's one thing we've never had to worry about on my island."

"You were born on Cliff Island?"

"Yep, born and raised. I spent a couple years in Portland for college but then went back. Not a real big traffic problem."

"So, if you don't mind my asking, where's Ella's dad? Is he waiting back home? Someone you met in Portland?"

"He's not waiting back home, that's for sure. His name

is Jack. He came to Cliff Island shortly after I'd moved back home. He said he wanted to experience "Island life". Well, I guess he experienced more than he bargained for and high-tailed it out of there when he found out I was pregnant."

"Asshole."

I shrugged.

"Didn't seem like it up to that point. I guess he got scared."

"Did he ever call? E-mail to find out how you were doing? Offer to help take care of Ella."

"Nope."

"Asshole."

I grinned.

"So do you have family? Anyone that can help when you get back?"

"My parents both died a few years back, that's why I went back to the island in the first place. No family, but lots of friends. I won't lack for help, that's for sure."

"Sorry about your parents."

I nodded.

Nurse Bell was quiet for a minute, cursed the traffic, and then fell silent again. Finally she took a deep breath and asked, "Did you ever worry that you'd be a horrible mother?"

"Every day," I replied without hesitation.

Nurse Bell glanced over at me, surprise evident in her wide eyes.

"Really?"

"Seriously," I answered earnestly. "I thought I'd be

awful. I felt like I would screw everything up, including her, which might still happen, but you know what? The one thing that I've learned through all of this is that she and I belong together. Without her it feels like there's a hole inside of me that nothing and no one else can fill. No matter how bad I mess up, no one else will love her as much as I do, and I think that's what every person needs more than anything else, someone to love them the most."

We spent the rest of the trip in silence until finally, what seemed like days later, we pulled into the Portland Main Medical Center parking garage. Nurse Bell's little electric roller-skate slid in between two other minis and she cut the engine.

"You wait here. They'll call the police if they scan you at the desk and your ID doesn't match. I'll go in and talk to Dr. Myers."

I sighed, but nodded in agreement.

Nurse Bell left and I waited. Eventually I adjusted my seat so that it reclined slightly, I rested my head and closed my eyes. Nurse Bell had cracked the windows, but not enough for adequate airflow. A hint of a breeze teased my hot face from time to time and I thought about getting out, but didn't know if it would be wise to wander. It didn't seem like anything too awful could happen in a hospital parking garage.

I nearly jumped out of my seat when I heard a knock on the window.

When I opened my eyes and turned to look, I saw Nurse Bell and, peering over her shoulder, none other than Dr. Myers. Nurse Bell had left the keys with me, so

I quickly unlocked the car and the two women slid inside. Nurse Bell gestured for Dr. Myers to take the front seat and she squeezed herself into the back.

Dr. Myers leaned forward and pulled me into a hug.

"Lana, I'm so relieved to see you." I was surprised but tried to return the embrace despite the awkward position.

The combination of her concern and just being in the arms of someone I had known before all of this happened opened the floodgates. In about thirty seconds I'd soaked the upper sleeve of her scrubs.

She held me until the sobs turned to sniffs and then gently pushed back and studied my face.

"Sorry," I said wiping tears from my face with my shirt sleeve, and then realized it was actually Nurse Bell's sleeve. "Sorry," I said again.

"You have nothing to apologize for," Dr. Myers stated. "Tell me what happened."

After a deep breath and a long exhale, I launched into the tale, trying to keep it brief and to the point. For most of the story my eyes were directed at the ceiling. I tried to picture the critical events and relay them to Dr. Myers. I wanted to make sure I included any details that might be relevant to her being able to help me.

When I reached the point about Dr. Ammon's assistant paying me a visit- was it really just that morning?- I glanced at her face to gauge her reaction and was shocked to see pure rage contort her normally pleasant features into the visage of someone no person would dare to cross. I actually faltered for a moment before hurrying to my providential encounter with Nurse Bell and our subsequent escape.

"So, here we are," I said in closing. "What do we do now?"

"The first thing we need to do is get you a new ID," Dr. Myers replied.

"You can do that?"

"Well, not by myself, but I can certainly speed up the process. This kind of thing doesn't happen often. At least, not under circumstances where the person in question is actually willing to come forth and admit that they are not, in fact, dead. Most illegals end up truly dead or in jail before anyone can help them. Then it can take months to get a physician to complete the necessary DNA tests to confirm the person's identity. I can do the tests for you, as well as confirm the majority of your story. That will help expedite the whole process and, hopefully, keep you out of jail."

"That would be really great," I replied, my voice flat and dry. "How long will it take?"

"Hopefully, no more than a week."

"A week!"

"I know, it seems like a long time, but while we're waiting for the ID, we can enlist some help in the search for Ella. Have you gone to the police?"

"No, not yet. We kind of wanted to get the ID thing squared away first."

"Good, I think that's a smart thing to do. Have you contacted anyone you know?"

"No, not yet, we've been a bit busy today."

Dr. Myers didn't respond to the sarcasm in my voice. She simply nodded and leaned forward and inch or two.

"Good. Don't contact anyone. You are on the records as having died and now you have a stolen ID. You will absolutely spend a night or two in jail while they try to sort it all out, and, if Dr. Ammon is looking for you, the first thing he'll do is access your contacts and see if you've called anyone."

Her words were like ice water poured over my skin. I felt goose bumps lift the hairs along both arms and send a shiver down my back.

"Do you have a place to stay while you wait?"

I glanced at Nurse Bell and raised my eyebrows.

"Yes, she's staying with me," Nurse Bell replied immediately, though as soon as she'd said the words, she began to chew on her lower lip.

"If it's going to cause a problem…" I began.

"No, no, you are more than welcome to stay, that's not what I'm worried about."

"What is it then?" Dr. Myers asked.

"Dr. Ammon," Nurse Bell replied. "When he goes back to the island and finds Lana and I gone, Rafael locked away, he's going to come looking. I'm afraid that my house might be the first place he looks. Unless I'm there, at the island…"

Dr. Myers glanced at her watch.

"I have to get back," she stated. "Please let me know what you decide to do, and Lana, give me your contact information the moment you know so that I can reach you to schedule the tests."

"Her cell was taken, so call mine and I'll relay messages. Here, I'm texting you my number." Nurse Bell typed rapidly with her thumbs and for about five seconds and looked up to confirm that the message went through.

Dr. Myers fished her phone out of her pants pocket and nodded.

"Keep in touch," she said before she opened the door and maneuvered gracefully from the driver's seat.

I watched her disappear down the nearest flight of stairs and I sighed.

A week, I thought miserably. In seven days my daughter could be anywhere in the world. If Dr. Ammon wanted to get rid of me, all he would have to do was hide Ella somewhere that I'd never find her. It would eventually kill me.

CHAPTER 14

FOR ONE RESTLESS night and one interminably long day, I hid in Nurse Bell's guest room. She'd tucked me away as soon as we'd returned from the hospital and informed me that she had to go back to the island, to wait for her here, and to stay hidden.

That night I kept the lights off and remained silent. My heart pounded in my throat every time I heard heavy footfalls down the hall. I don't know why I feared Nurse Bell's husband. Perhaps it was that he knew Dr. Ammon and might tell him where I was. Perhaps it was Nurse Bell's insistence that I stay hidden. Either way, I barely slept and tried not to move until I heard the faint sound of an electric engine pulling out of the driveway the next morning.

Finally, when I felt certain he would not return, I slept.

When I woke the sun streamed in the east facing windows, making hot patches on the covers. I dared take a shower and then tiptoed out of the bedroom and into the kitchen.

The refrigerator had been stocked with fresh fruits, vegetables, and even a carton of eggs. My mouth drooled at the thought of scrambled eggs, but I didn't want to dirty any dishes, or throw away egg shells and leave behind evidence of my stay. I closed the fridge and rifled through the cupboards until I found a chocolate protein bar.

It didn't taste like chocolate, that's for sure. More like wax. It stopped my stomach from growling at me though. I finished the bar, tucked the wrapper into my borrowed pants pocket, and then paced the living room and stared out to sea.

On my third tour of the room, I spied a tablet which, thank the stars above, was charged and full of books. I snatched up the device and hurried back to the guest room where I managed to successfully pass the rest of the day with only the occasional moment of restless panic.

The sun had long since abandoned my side of the house when the door to the guest room zipped open and I bolted upright.

"Time to go," Nurse Bell announced before she turned and disappeared behind the wall.

After scooting off the edge of the bed, I turned and tried to smooth out the wrinkles so that it wouldn't look slept in. It turned out to be an impossible task. No matter how much I smoothed and tucked, it refused to return to its original state of perfection. I suspected that, before my visit, it really had never been used.

"Come on!" Nurse Bell reappeared in the doorway,

hands on hips. For the first time since I'd met her, Nurse Bell looked tired and disheveled.

Abandoning my attempts at restoring the bed to its original state, I slid on a pair of borrowed shoes and looked up with a grimace. I hadn't asked about the pants, or the shoes. Fortunately Lacy nodded and waved me along.

"Where are we going?" I asked as we headed back out to the docks.

"I'm not sure yet, but we can't stay here."

"Why not? What's going on?"

"I'm not entirely certain about that either. Something bigger than we realized, that's for sure."

"What do you mean?"

Nurse Bell didn't respond immediately. I followed all the way to the boat, where Nurse Bell hopped in and began to deftly unknot ropes and throw them into the bottom of the boat. Once she fired up the engine, I asked again.

"What do you mean, 'something bigger than we realized'?"

Nurse Bell looked me straight in the eye and said, "They're married."

A frown creased my brow. I tried, and failed, to figure out who she might be referring to.

"Dr. Ammon and Dr. Myers!" she yelled. "They're married!"

My jaw actually dropped.

"What?!?"

"Dr. Ammon and-"

"No, I mean yes, I heard you, but how is that possible?"

"Well, apparently they met a looong time ago, fell in love, and had this little ceremony where a priest-"

"Hey!"

Nurse Bell took a deep breath and let it out in a huff.

"Sorry, I've just been going crazy ever since I found out." Nurse Bell twisted her hands on the steering wheel before she pounded it with a fist.

My eyebrows lifted in surprise. I'd never seen Lacy Bell so mad.

"Sorry," she said again, catching my expression.

"No, no need to apologize, you've had a lot longer to stew on it." In fact, the more I thought about it, the more confused I became.

"How did you find out?"

Nurse Bell's expression shifted from fierce to apologetic in a heartbeat.

"I talked to Rafael."

"Oh," I replied. I pushed myself back against the seat and pulled Nurse Bell's borrowed hoodie tighter around my torso, tucking each hand under the opposite arm for good measure.

"I needed to talk to him about pass codes for Dr. Ammon's office and files. I wanted to see if I could find out where he'd taken Ella." She paused and I nodded encouragingly.

"That sounds like a good idea. Did he tell you what you needed to know?"

"Well, he did, eventually...but for a price."

I could actually feel the goose bumps form along my arms and shoulders.

"And…"

"And I had to let him out."

The cold chill which had raised the goose bumps settled into the pit of my stomach and hardened into a block of ice. My gaze shifted to the sea and I cast my eyes out across the horizon, trying to catch a glimpse of any boats that might be pursuing us down the coastline.

"I'm so sorry. That was his condition for helping and I thought it was more important to get that information. He did get me into Dr. Ammon's office and I managed to access his files. While I was digging around I found this." She unzipped her right coat pocket and pulled out a clear cylinder. Suspended inside was an ID chip.

I gasped and reached for it, then paused and glanced at Nurse Bell for confirmation.

She responded with a triumphant smile.

"I scanned it to make sure. It's you." With that she leaned forward and handed me my ID. "There's one other thing for you in there." Nurse Bell nodded to one of the seats, which were hollow underneath the padded top cushion for storage. I opened the lid and almost started to cry when I saw my bags tucked down inside.

With shaking fingers, I pulled one bag out of the tiny storage compartment and plopped it on my lap. I fished through the contents, thankful to have a few outfits that might actually fit me. I continued to shift and dig, hoping against hope that my phone may have magically materialized, but no such luck. The pieces were coming back together though. I had my ID and I was off the island.

I started to feel a thrill of hope that I just might be able to put my life back together. All I needed now was Ella.

"Thank you!" I yelled.

I wanted to hug her, but not badly enough to risk being tossed overboard in the choppy sea.

She smiled and nodded.

"So, while I was digging through his desk for your ID, I found a picture of him and Dr. Myers…a wedding picture! I pulled it out and must have stared at it for five minutes before Rafael crept up behind me and said, "I bet he never told you he was married, did he?"

I could see Nurse Bell shuddering slightly at the memory.

"I didn't want to believe him but, well, it was kind of staring me in the face."

I nodded, mostly because I had no idea what to say, or what to do with this piece of information.

"I can't believe he let you go!" I said finally. "And with my ID!"

Nurse Bell grimaced before she answered.

"Well, it was all part of the deal I made with him. See, he needs his back too."

"Ahh, so he hasn't suddenly become altruistic after all."

Nurse Bell scoffed.

A thought occurred to me, and on the heels of this thought, a cold knot began to form in my gut.

"So, is that where we're going? To meet him somewhere?"

"No! Oh my gosh, no!" I exhaled in relief and waited

for Nurse Bell to continue. "We're going to go somewhere safe, to someone who can switch out the IDs, then I'll return Rafael's to him by myself."

"What about you? Won't it be dangerous for you to go back there again? What if Dr. Ammon is there? Do you think Rafael has already contacted him?"

Nurse Bell lifted her eyebrows.

"I'm guessing his *wife* has already informed him of our whereabouts."

"Oh, right." I still couldn't quite believe that piece of information. Dr. Ammon had left the island to visit the mainland for a couple of days, and we'd gone straight to his wife for help. Had she already known everything that had happened? I couldn't imagine her being okay with any of this. She'd always seemed so friendly, so genuinely concerned about me and my baby-

"How could she?" I said and balled my hands into fists.

"What?" Nurse Bell yelled.

"Dr. Myers, she had to have known all along!"

Nurse Bell raised her eyebrows again.

"Ya think?"

"No, I mean I think she planned this all along!"

"What? Why?"

"After my very first ultrasound, she was showing me one of the pictures and explaining what everything was and she said, 'You're so lucky. She looks perfect. I'd give anything to have my own baby girl.' Then she stared at the picture for a while before she left." I sat there, hugging my bag while I replayed the scene in my mind. I felt stunned and horrified, but I also felt a sense of anticipation. A small beam of light had finally started to shine through this big black hole of what my life had become. "I think she has Ella."

Nurse Bell watched me, but didn't respond.

We sat in silence for a while, each of us lost in our own tangle of thoughts until, after another twenty minutes or so, Nurse Bell turned toward shore and pulled alongside another dock.

"A friend of mine lives here," she explained in response to my quizzical look. "I think he'll be able to help us."

I helped her secure the boat to the dock before we climbed two sets of stairs up to the house.

"Won't he be at work right now?"

"He should be home. He works nights."

"Well, then, won't he be asleep?"

"Maybe," she admitted. "But I think this is worth waking him up for."

Nurse Bell marched up to the front door and pressed a button, then waited.

"What does he do?" I asked, wondering if Nurse Bell planned to enlist him to help find Ella.

"He's a Doctor."

I froze.

"A Doctor? Why would I need to go to another Doctor?" Quite frankly, I'd had more than enough of Doctors.

Before she could answer, I saw movement through the glass door. Lacy waved to a man who approached wearing pajama pants and a waffle-knit shirt. His dark hair was tousled and he scrubbed one hand over his face before he placed it on the door handle.

When he saw Nurse Bell on the other side of the glass, the man grinned, revealing straight and slightly off-white teeth. I guessed it took a lot of coffee to work nights. He pulled open the door.

"Lacy!" he exclaimed and pulled her into a hug. He seemed genuinely happy to see her despite the fact that he'd obviously been asleep.

Lacy stepped into his embrace and out again quickly.

"Simon! It's great to see you," she said. She stepped back and then spread one hand toward me. "This is my friend, Lana."

"Hi, Lana, it's a pleasure to meet you." Simon's smile shifted to me and he extended one hand in greeting.

"Nice to meet you, too," I replied. I began to extend my right hand, belatedly realizing I held my ID in its clear case. I felt my cheeks grow warm. I shifted the case to my left hand and finally took his in greeting.

Simon continued to smile, but his eyes flicked to the case briefly before returning to my face.

"To what do I owe this pleasure?" he asked before he released my hand and stepped back, gesturing for us to come inside.

"We need your help," Nurse Bell declared as she stepped through the doorway.

I followed, still somewhat tentative about revealing the whole story to this stranger. I glanced around the modest house and noticed there were few decorations, but lots of books, real paper books. That's when I began to trust Simon.

"Can I get you anything to drink?" Simon asked.

"No, thanks," Nurse Bell replied, then glanced at me with raised eyebrows.

"No thanks," I echoed. I sat on the edge of one of the chairs across from the couch, running a thumb along the curve of the ID case or alternately tucking my hair behind my ears.

"Well, what can I help with?" He asked before settling onto the faux leather couch.

Nurse Bell glanced at me, and then turned toward Simon.

"Lana needs her ID chip reinserted…" Nurse Bell paused and waited for Simon's reaction. His eyes widened slightly and he glanced at the clear case in my hands, but then he simply nodded. "And we need to get into the hospital's maternity ward."

Simon's eyebrows lifted this time and my head jerked toward Nurse Bell. She hadn't mentioned *where* Simon worked nights.

Then they both turned to look at me. At first I squirmed under the dual scrutiny, and then decided to stop wasting time and cut to the chase.

"Do you want the long version or the short version?" I asked.

"How about the short version first, then fill in the details once I know whether or not I can help."

So, he hadn't decided if he would or not yet. I guess it was wise of him to be cautious.

"The short version is that Dr. Ammon stole my baby and my ID before he locked me in a room on the island where Nurse Bell works. I stole the ID from his assistant, got out of the room, ran into Nurse Bell, literally, and we got out of there. Now I have my ID back but someone still has my baby."

Simon stared at me for a full minute, his dark brown eyes unreadable. Finally, he leaned forward and held out one hand.

"Let me take a look at your hand."

I placed the back of my right hand into the palm of his left and uncurled my fingers. With his right index finger, he gently traced the thin red line where I'd reopened the original incision on my palm with a piece of glass. The skin around the cut was red and I winced when he put gentle pressure on the wound.

"There's a bit of infection. I'll need to clean it up after I reopen the cut."

A long exhale of relief fled from my lungs. I hadn't even realized I'd been holding my breath.

Simon's eyes met mine, clearly wondering about the rest of the story, but he didn't ask. I didn't offer.

"So you'll help us?" Nurse Bell asked.

"Yes, with the ID for sure. It may take a little more work to get you into the hospital, but I'll see what I can do. I wish I could do more."

"Well..." Nurse Bell began. Simon and I both turned our attention to her. She tugged at her shirt sleeves. "There might be something more you could do."

"Oh?" Simon asked. A small smile tugged at the corners of his mouth.

I frowned, wondering what Lacy Bell had cooking up now.

"She needs a safe place to stay while I return the other ID chip, and hopefully get a few more answers. It's not safe for her to go with me, not that I think she'd want to, and I don't feel like leaving her at my house again is safe either." Simon frowned, prompting Nurse Bell to continue. "When we first arrived on the mainland we went to see Dr. Myers. She was Lana's OB up until she sent her to the island for her delivery. Dr. Ammon, the one who took her baby, is married to Dr. Myers. I never knew that."

Simon frowned.

"I didn't know that either," he replied. "Are you sure?"

"I saw their wedding picture, and it didn't look that old."

"So, do you think they're looking for you?" he addressed this question to me, all I could do was shrug.

"They are or they will be soon," Nurse Bell declared. "And the guy whose ID she took to escape agreed to help me in order to get his own ID back. Once he gets it I have no doubt he'll come looking."

I shivered and wrapped my free arm around myself. Simon must have felt my reaction through the hand that he still held. He turned to look at me, and then he gently squeezed my right hand before he released it.

"Lacy, I don't think you should go back. We should go to the police, give Rafael's ID to them, tell them everything that happened, and maybe they can find Ella." I was tired of the games, tired of hiding, and I didn't want to involve Simon in my mess.

"I made a promise," Lacy responded.

I sighed and closed my eyes briefly before fixing them again on Lacy Bell.

"Lacy, you made a promise to a man with no morals, a man who stole my baby and tried to rape me. I really don't think you should go back there alone and I sure as hell don't want to give him the means to come after me."

"I know, I know, but if Rafael has his ID he can access all the files with a scan and passcode, which I still don't know. I can find out the name and address of the woman who left with Dr. Ammon. Maybe *she* has Ella. Maybe we won't even have to go to the hospital."

Lacy paced and wrapped her arms around herself.

"That's pretty weak. Is that all you've got?" I asked.

She stopped and faced me, then shook her head.

"I want to know why. I want to know what's really going on and why I never knew he was married."

"Because he's a jerk with too much money and no one holding him accountable?" I speculated.

One corner of Nurse Bell's mouth twitched in a half smile.

"I'm pretty sure the police can ask all those questions." Simon spoke softly.

Nurse Bell continued to pace and didn't respond. She seemed to be lost in her own thoughts.

Simon turned to me and tipped his head.

"Come with me. We'll give her some time to think while we take care of that hand."

Nurse Bell continued to pace. Simon led me to a back bathroom. He paused at the door.

"Uh, just give me one second," he said.

He ducked into the bathroom with a sheepish grin and I couldn't help but smile when I heard the clink of a toothbrush being placed in a cup. This was followed by the pop of a medicine cabinet and the screech of shower curtain rings along a metal curtain rod. Finally, I heard the creak and then thump of a clothes hamper.

My grin widened when the door opened and Simon beckoned me inside.

"I don't get a lot of female company," Simon explained.

"That's hard to believe." The words came out before I'd even consciously processed the thought. A blush warmed my face.

Simon chuckled.

"Well, not for lack of trying, but it's tough to get a date when you work ten to twelve hours overnight and sleep most of the day."

"Yeah, sorry we woke you."

"Oh, no problem, I was just getting up." He waved away the apology and then began to open drawers and cabinets. He gathered and set out various implements that made my stomach flip-flop. "I'm so sorry about your daughter and, well, all of it." Simon paused and looked straight at me, concern evident on his face.

I felt tears well up and threaten to spill, forcing me to look away and bit the inside of my cheek. I didn't trust my voice at the moment, so I simply nodded in response.

"Here, you sit on the tub." Simon nodded toward the blue tile which rose on either side of the tub and then formed a flat ledge at knee height. I sat on the tub as instructed. Simon took a seat on the lid of the toilet.

He rested a tray on the edge of the sink. On the tray he'd neatly laid out a scalpel, tweezers, gauze, a tube of something whose label I could not see clearly, and q-tips. Beside the tray he set a bottle of disinfectant. He scanned his assortment one last time before he held out his hand and nodded toward my right.

Again I placed my hand in his.

It's amazing how such a simple touch can provide so much comfort.

Sitting there, in that tiny bathroom watching Simon brush an antiseptic-soaked swab across my palm was the safest I'd felt in a long time.

As the liquid worked its way past the adhesive and down into the wound, I sucked air between my teeth. Simon bent his head over my palm and blew on the bubbles, just like my mother used to do.

Butterflies seemed to cartwheel through my stomach as his breath tickled my skin. He smelled like pine.

I didn't even realize I'd leaned in closer until he picked his head up and nearly smashed into my nose. Instinctively, I pulled back a little too fast and nearly slipped backwards off the edge of the tub. My free hand went down to catch me at the same time that Simon's right hand gripped my leg and his left hand tightened around my own.

"You okay?" he asked.

I blushed again and nodded.

"Sorry."

He grinned and the butterflies went wild.

"You need to stop apologizing so much."

"Sor-" I caught myself and pressed my lips together. Simon began to laugh.

I couldn't help but laugh too. It felt good.

"I think that's the first time I've laughed in a month," I said, once I'd caught my breath.

Immediately, I regretted my words when Simon's eyebrows pulled together and his expression turned serious.

"I just can't believe someone would do that to you. I mean, I believe you, but it's all so crazy." He paused and shook his head. "I can't imagine what you've been through."

He gave my hand a gentle squeeze and the laughter inside of me died. The familiar lump returned to my throat. I sat silently while he examined my hand.

"Okay, next is some betadine," he said seconds before smearing the dark orange liquid across my palm. "And now some numbing cream." His thumb made gentle circles around the meat of my hand until I could no longer feel the contact.

"Numb yet?" he asked and glanced up.

I nodded, wishing there was such a thing as numbing cream for the heart. A heart that started to pound when Simon picked up the surgical scalpel.

He must have felt my hand tense because he stopped and looked at me. He spoke in the kind of voice that people use on distressed animals.

"The numbing cream works fast," he assured me. "And the cut will be shallow. I promise I won't hurt you."

I inhaled through my nose, forcing my hand to relax. The rest of my body tensed when the blade approached my skin. I watched the knife go in, I watched a thin line of blood well from the cut, but I didn't feel anything. My shoulders began to relax ever so slightly.

"You're doing great. I'm done with the incision, now I'm going to remove the chip that's in there and put your ID back in, okay?"

I nodded, enjoying the confident, calm, clinical tone of his voice. I tried counting my breaths as I inhaled and exhaled. My eyes stayed fixed on the top of his head while he worked. I couldn't help but wonder if this is how the fish felt when I slapped them down on my cutting board and stunned them before slicing them open.

"So, how did you get this guy's ID out of him and into you?" Simon asked as he set Rafael's chip, still inside the clear casing, carefully on the tray using one pair of tweezers.

"I used a piece of broken glass to cut it out of his hand," I replied.

Simon looked at me and raised his eyebrows, then nodded in appreciation.

I have to admit, it even surprised me. I hadn't thought much about it at the time, I'd been running on adrenaline and desperation, it had been necessary. I think I avoided thinking about it since.

"Did you tie him up first?" he asked mildly before he returned to his task.

The fact that he hadn't overreacted, hadn't judged my actions, made it easier to tell him more.

"No, I knocked him out."

Simon nodded and said, "Good for you."

I chuckled.

"It's hard to believe I did any of that. I can't even watch you right now, but somehow I managed to slice him open, and dig out his ID. Oh, and Nurse Bell helped me with getting it placed in my palm after she found me so that we could get out of the building without raising suspicion."

"You must have been pretty scared."

Simon placed my hand across his knees. He removed Rafael's chip from the casing and replaced it with mine.

"Yeah," was all I said.

He picked up a thin, flat tool with his left hand and retrieved the encased ID with a clean pair of tweezers. He paused with both hands poised over my open palm.

"I promise this won't hurt. Are you ready?"

I swallowed and then nodded.

Simon pushed the long, flat tool into the incision and gently lifted the top layer of skin. He slipped the protected ID into the slit and held it in place with the tweezers as he pulled out the flat tool.

"Did *he* hurt you?" Simon's hands stopped moving when he asked this, but he didn't look at me.

It took me a moment to realize which *he* Simon referred to.

"Physically? Nothing that won't heal, but he was the one who took Ella from my arms the last time I saw her. I wanted to kill him."

Simon nodded slowly and then his hands began to move again. He placed his tools on the tray, then washed and dried his hands before picking up a tube of adhesive.

"That's understandable," he said. I watched Simon squeeze a line of gel along the fresh cut. "Why didn't you?"

The question surprised me.

"I don't know, I just couldn't I guess. I mean, I probably wouldn't have shed a tear if it had happened by accident but to do it on purpose, while he's just lying there," I paused and shook my head. "I could never do that."

Simon nodded.

"And you're done," he declared. "You were a model patient."

I smiled.

A moment of comfortable silence passed. We continued to sit there, neither one moving to go.

Simon opened his mouth to speak, but before any words came out, the sound of a fist pounding on the door made us both jump.

"Lana? Are you done?" Nurse Bell opened the door and poked her head through the crack. She glanced from me to Simon and back. "My husband tried to call twice but didn't leave a message, then he sent me a text, he never texts. I'm pretty sure someone got a hold of him and is trying to find me…us."

"What do we do now?" I asked.

"You call the police," Simon stated in a not-open-for-discussion kind of voice.

Nurse Bell sighed.

"All right, all right, one sec." And she disappeared again.

"Do you want something to drink?" Simon asked.

"Sure," I replied.

I followed him out of the bathroom and back to the kitchen where Nurse Bell had resumed her pacing, but was now also holding her phone to her ear.

She glanced over when we entered the room, moved her phone in front of her face, and then tapped the screen before she returned it to her ear.

"Damn automated answering systems," she announced.

I scoffed and shook my head.

"It's a wonder more people don't die on hold, waiting to talk to a real person."

Simon smiled and pulled two glasses from a cupboard.

"Lacy Bell, calling to report a...missing child." She glanced at me and shrugged. I shrugged back, and then nodded. "That's Lacy Bell, 1325-629-10207, please call back immediately."

She pressed a thumb to the end call button and seemed barely able to restrain herself from throwing the phone across the room.

"They'll call back as soon as there's an available case worker," she announced.

"Water?" Simon asked, offering a glass to Nurse Bell.

She took it, guzzled it, and began pacing again.

"Aren't I the one who should be stressed out?" I asked, watching Nurse Bell. She marched, spun on her heel, and marched again.

"What if I'm implicated in this? I mean, I work there! Well, worked there. Which means I have no job! What if I can't find another job?"

"Try not to freak out," I said calmly. "It's not good for the baby."

Nurse Bell stopped, looked at me with wide eyes and placed both hands on her abdomen. Without a word she plunked down in the nearest chair and stared out the window.

"Lacy, you're pregnant?!?" Simon waited for her nod then walked over, sat beside her and wrapped an arm around her shoulders, giving her an affectionate squeeze. "Congratulations."

Inwardly, I cringed. That's probably something I should have let her announce to her friends.

She smiled and patted on of Simon's hands. Then she turned to look at me. I expected some sort of reprimand.

"Well, what do you want to do next, Lana?"

"Find Ella," was, of course, the first thing that popped out of my mouth.

"I know," Nurse Bell replied softly, "But we need a plan."

I glanced out the window and noticed the sun sparkling off the water in that muted late-afternoon way that didn't hurt your eyes when you stared at the reflection. It was getting late. Simon would have to go to work.

"I think Lana should wait here, if that's okay with you, Simon." Nurse Bell glanced at him for confirmation and continued after he nodded. "We wait for the police to call back while Simon goes in to work and sees if there's a way to get us into the maternity ward, or to find out who is there. First thing in the morning we either go talk to the police or go into the hospital, depending on tonight's outcome."

I rubbed my right thumb into the joint at the base of my left thumb like a worry stone. I didn't like this plan at all. I wanted to go to the hospital with Simon tonight. I wanted to go straight to the police station, which would be closed by now anyway, and pound on the door until someone agreed to help me find my baby.

"I may need to check in at home first, but Lana, you should stay here. I'll meet you back here as soon as I've made my appearance. Agreed?"

"What if the police call you back?" I asked.

"I'll make an appointment to talk to them tomorrow."

I sighed a deep sigh, searching for patience, and finally nodded.

"Tomorrow then."

Nurse Bell nodded and stood.

"I'm going to head back while it's still light. I'll call if there's any news." She paused and then asked. "Can I just use your bathroom first?"

"Of course," Simon replied gesturing down the hall to the place where he'd just performed minor surgery.

"Thanks."

Once Nurse Bell returned to the living room, her phone rang. We all jumped and crowded around to see whose name came up on the caller ID.

"Dr. Myers." Nurse Bell said the name aloud even though we could all read it. Her eyes met mine and I nodded toward the phone.

"Hello?" she said after she pressed the green answer

button. She listened for several seconds, nodded, and then replied, "Yes, I think that will work. Let me get in touch with her and I'll call you back."

A few more seconds and then she hung up the phone.

"Well?" I asked. She stood there, staring at the screen.

Finally, Nurse Bell looked up and said, "She wants you to come in for an appointment tomorrow at one'o'clock."

Silence.

"Do you think she knows what's going on?" Simon asked.

"She has to," Nurse Bell replied. "How could she not know? I say we go to the appointment and once we're in, that's our chance to look around. Simon, maybe you could try to find out tonight who has checked in over the past couple of days, and then tomorrow, while Lana is keeping Dr. Myers busy, we'll see about finding Ella."

Nurse Bell and Simon both looked at me.

I nodded.

Nurse Bell left. Simon left. Alone in the unfamiliar house, I paced until long after dark. Eventually I must have gone to sleep, because I woke up on the couch just as the sun began to show its face at the start of a new day.

By the time Simon returned, I was showered, had eaten breakfast, and had just sat down with my second cup of coffee.

"Good morning," Simon greeted me as he walked into the kitchen. His voice sounded tired.

"Good morning," I replied. "There's more coffee if you want some. How was work?"

"Busy," he answered, "Which is good for making the

time go by a bit faster, but not so good for helping you out. I did look up a list of new patient registrations over the last four days, and there were two new infants checked in. Neither by the name of Ella Wexler, but I would imagine, if they put her in the database at all, they would've changed her name."

"Changed her name?" The thought horrified me. She was my daughter. My flesh and blood whom I had named. They had no right to change that. Then again, they had no right to take her from me, what would stop them from changing her identity.

A knock at the door interrupted my train of thought. I looked up to see Nurse Bell outside the glass doors on the ocean side. She had a thin jacket wrapped around her with her hands tucked under her armpits. Simon hurried to let her inside.

"Morning!" she called as she entered, cheery and not a hair out of place even after a boat ride across the ocean this early in the day.

"Morning," I replied. "Did you hear back from the police?"

"Not yet," Nurse Bell replied, "But I did find out some important news."

"What?" I asked, sitting up a little straighter in my chair.

"I found the name and address of the woman who left with Dr. Ammon, the one who was carrying Ella."

CHAPTER 15

"You found her! Who is she? Where is she?" I stood and abandoned my mug of coffee, striding toward Nurse Bell in my excitement to find out the news.

"Her name is Marjorie, Marjorie Englestine, and here's where she lives," Nurse Bell held her phone out so that I could see the map. "It's about thirty five minutes north and west of here. We could try calling-"

"No," I interrupted and cut one hand through the air for emphasis. "We are going there *right, now.*"

Nurse Bell and Simon exchanged a glance.

"If we leave right now, traffic won't be too bad," Simon stated.

"We?" Nurse Bell asked, raising her eyebrows.

Simon looked at me, then back to Nurse Bell, and nodded.

Nurse Bell cocked one eyebrow, but made no comment. Instead she returned her phone to the home screen and slid it into a coat pocket.

"Well, what are we waiting for?"

I nodded and then dumped the remainder of my coffee down the drain before placing my mug in the sink. Simon poured his coffee into a travel mug then offered some to Nurse Bell.

"I'd love to but…no thanks." She placed a hand over her abdomen.

"Oh…right." Simon smiled and turned off the coffee maker, then led the way to the garage.

As I followed on his heels, all of the anxiety and restlessness which had been simmering just below the surface came rushing in times ten.

She was so close. In thirty-five minutes I might hold my baby girl in my arms again.

Might, I repeated. I had to remind myself she might not be there, but I couldn't stop my heart from yearning.

Except for the fact that Simon's car was forest green, it was in all other ways identical to Nurse Bell's: tiny and electric with a roof that doubled as a solar panel.

Nurse Bell offered me the front seat but I shook my head.

"You take it. You can help navigate."

Nurse Bell shrugged and pulled up the seat so that I could climb into the back. I immediately regretted my decision. The space had clearly been designed for children or grocery bags, not five-foot seven-inch post-partum women. I had to turn my legs sideways so that my torso angled behind Simon's seat and my feet rested behind Nurse Bell's.

Thirty-five minutes, I thought to myself.

As Simon reached for the garage door opener, I felt compelled to say, "You know, Simon, you really don't need to do this. I don't want you to end up in mess, or out of a job, because you helped me."

Simon nodded thoughtfully.

"I do have to actually. I couldn't live with myself if I sat around and did nothing when I might have been able to help so, here we go."

With that he zipped down the long driveway, barely pausing before he turned onto the main road which would connect us to the highway.

"So, Lacy, how did you acquire this very helpful piece of information?" Simon asked once we'd established our place in the flow of traffic.

Nurse Bell looked out the passenger side window and responded. "I went back to the Island."

Simon nodded. "I thought as much when I discovered the ID missing from the bathroom." His tone was accusatory.

"Hey, I got what we needed didn't I?"

"But now he has his ID," I said softly.

"Actually, he doesn't. Well, he does, but I didn't give it to him," Nurse Bell responded.

"What do you mean?" I asked.

Nurse Bell held up a clear disc with an ID inside.

"I didn't have to give it to him, he already had a new one."

"That was fast," Simon muttered.

"Then why did he help you?" I asked.

"Good question," Nurse Bell replied and furrowed her brow. She clearly hadn't thought about that.

"Maybe because the information he gave you wouldn't help us," Simon guessed.

"Or maybe so that he would know where to find us," I added.

Silence hung thick in the cramped interior until Simon attempted to get the conversation moving again.

"So, how did this woman end up with your baby?" he asked, glancing at me in the rear view mirror.

"Well, Dr. Ammon and Rafael took Ella and locked me away. I don't really know what happened after that." I looked at Nurse Bell for more of the story.

"I'm not totally sure either." Nurse Bell picked up the story. "I came back from leave and Dr. Ammon told me that Lana and Ella had drowned when their boat capsized in a storm on the way home. Then I saw this woman, Marjorie, who'd been expecting her baby any day when I'd left. Well, by the time I returned, she'd had her baby and the baby looked just like Ella. At the time I didn't have any reason to question it. A day or two after I returned, they left for the mainland, that was actually the first time I saw her with Ella. I never thought twice about it, until Lana ran into me in the hallway all torn up and bloody."

It was interesting to hear her description of events, and of me when she'd first seen me. Hard to believe that had only been two days ago. It felt more like a year.

The thirty-five minutes it took to drive from Simon's sea-side home to the green blip on the GPS were among the most wonderful and most agonizing of my life. I would intermittently picture Ella's face and imagine holding her. This would, of course, start the tears and, blinking them away, I would try to think of something else, something that wouldn't get my hopes up. Naturally, I would end up imagining that she was not there, or that something awful had happened to her. My eyes would fill with more tears and in an effort to return to a place of hope, I would imagine holding her again. The imagination is a powerful and sometimes terrible thing. The not knowing threatened to tear me apart. The endless battle of needing to hope and needing to grieve, but not allowing myself to fully give in to either emotion, exhausted every last cell of my mind, body, and soul.

From time to time I caught Simon glancing at me in the rearview mirror and I would immediately look away. My composure was a fragile thing and I knew if I let myself accept his sympathy, the shell would crack, I'd never be able to hold it together.

As the dots on the GPS drew closer together, I leaned forward to get a better view of the houses. We turned into an apartment complex, and it turns out Marjorie's house was in fact one of the units on the ground floor of the second of four identical buildings.

My heart hammered as Simon pulled into a parking spot in front of the building. My hands actually began to shake. I gripped the sides of the front seat to try to stop the involuntary movement.

"You okay?" Simon asked. "You can wait here if you want. We can go knock, see if she's even there."

I knew he was trying to spare me a public meltdown, but there was no chance I would be waiting in the car.

"No, I have to go."

Simon nodded and Nurse Bell slid out. She turned and held the seat forward so that I could do the same. We stepped onto the sidewalk. She and Simon flanked me like two bookends, holding me up by the strength of their will.

Nurse Bell pushed the button below the apartment number and I heard the three chimes announcing our arrival.

Inhaling through my nose and exhaling through my mouth, I waited for someone to open the door, barely able to resist the urge to start pounding on the door with both fists.

When the door finally opened, I blinked, looked down, and blinked again.

A young girl, about seven or eight, stood on the opposite side of the threshold, holding the doorknob. She smiled up at us.

"Hello," she greeted us in a friendly but tentative voice.

"Uh, hi," said Simon, apparently the first one to recover from his shock. "My name is Simon. These are my friends, Lana and Lacy. We were hoping to talk to your mom. Is your mom home?"

The girl nodded and disappeared behind the half-closed door. A moment later I heard her call, "Mom, someone's here to see you!"

She sounded far away. We could have walked right

in through the open door and all I could think was that someone really needed to teach this girl about safety.

We remained on the doorstep, waiting. After a few minutes, I heard two sets of footsteps approaching. I started to twist the hem of my shirt between my fingers.

The little girl reappeared, holding on to a hand. Another hand began to pull the door open and I held my breath. The woman revealed herself inch by inch, and I frowned.

Glancing over at Nurse Bell, I saw the same look of confusion on her face. This did not look like a woman who'd just had a baby. In fact, this did not look like a woman who'd ever had a baby. She looked like she could stand to gain ten or fifteen pounds.

"How can I help you?" she asked. Her eyes scanned us warily and she pulled her daughter by the shoulder until she stood slightly behind the woman.

"We're looking for Marjorie Englestein. Do you know her?"

The woman's eyes narrowed.

"Who wants to know?"

"Sorry, my name's Lacy Bell, I was a nurse at the hospital where Marjorie went to have her baby. I'm checking up on her, and my friend Lana was also a patient there."

The woman's shoulders relaxed a little. She leaned down and whispered in her daughter's ear. The little girl smiled and then ran down the hallway.

"Yes, I know her, but she's not here right now." My heart sank. "She called and said she was transferred due to some *complications*." She directed her statement at Nurse

Bell and then cocked her head, clearly hoping to get some answers of her own.

I didn't hear Nurse Bell's response. My mind reeled. *She's not here. Is she at the hospital? Does Marjorie still have her? Where did Dr. Ammon take her? Which hospital?*

I bit my lip to keep from crying, then I felt Simon's hand slide into mine and squeeze. I squeezed back, maybe a little too hard. It was nice to have something to hold on to.

"Well, thank you." I heard Nurse Bell say. "Sorry to have disturbed you."

"No problem. If you see her you tell her to call me, okay?"

"I will," Nurse Bell replied, gave the woman a smile, and turned to go.

Simon and I followed.

Once all the doors were closed, we sat, wondering what to do next.

"I think-"

"Let's-"

"We should-"

We all started at once, stopped, and looked at each other.

"Lana, you go first," Simon decided.

"I think we should go the hospital," I stated.

"It's only eleven'o'clock," Nurse Bell replied.

"I think I should take you to the police right now, maybe they can go with you to your appointment at one." Simon glanced between me and Nurse Bell.

Nurse Bell stared out the window, chewing on her lip.

"What's the matter?" I asked.

"I can't stop wondering, where is Dr. Ammon? I mean, he's the one responsible for this. Why would he want to take Ella and where did he go? He wasn't back at the island when I went back there, so what's he doing?"

"I bet Dr. Myers would know. Yet another reason to go to the hospital," I declared.

"Do you really think she'd tell us?" Nurse Bell retorted.

Sighing heavily, I met Simon's eyes in the mirror.

"All right, let's go to the police." I sat back and crossed my arms. I felt like I was literally trying to hold myself together, that if I didn't find Ella soon, I might come unglued, unhinged, all those perfectly apt descriptors of someone truly falling apart.

Simon didn't waste any time. He fired up the engine and backed the car out of the space to the sound of an electric whir that reminded me of one of those toys where you pulled the zip line out and let it go.

We were barely out on the main road when Nurse Bell's cell began to ring, an old-fashioned telephone ringtone.

She didn't pick it up right away and when I looked at her face, I knew something was wrong.

"Who is it?" I asked.

"Dr. Ammon."

No one spoke for several seconds. Nurse Bell finally picked up the phone.

"Hello?" Nurse Bell made a valiant effort to sound normal, but I could hear the tension in her voice.

I heard the low rumble of a response, but I couldn't

make out the words. Nurse Bell swallowed and the color drained from her face.

My fingers curled around the seat and squeezed, but I dared not talk for fear of Dr. Ammon hearing my voice.

"Yes, I'll tell him," Nurse Bell stated, then added, "About ten minutes."

As she tapped her screen to hang up the phone, I could see her finger shaking.

"What is it? What did he say?" I asked.

"Simon, you need to take the next exit, turn right off the exit and drive three miles, take a left and continue to the free clinic."

"What? Why?" Simon asked.

"Just do it," Nurse Bell replied.

"I am not going to drive somewhere because this wackjob told me to. I'm going to the police station."

"No, you are going to the free clinic," Nurse Bell stared at Simon and spoke in a voice that allowed no argument.

"Why?" Simon asked.

Nurse Bell glanced back at me briefly, then turned her attention back to Simon.

"Because if you don't, he'll hurt Ella."

CHAPTER 16

"Hurt Ella! Does he have Ella? Is she at this free clinic?"
I practically climbed into the front seat as I questioned
Nurse Bell.

"I don't think he has her and I don't know if she's at
the clinic."

"If you don't think he has her, how could he hurt her?
What did he say?"

"He said all it would take was one phone call."

My chest started to tighten painfully.

"One phone call to whom," I choked out the words,
hardly able to think about who might have my daughter.
Someone who would be willing to hurt her with no more
than a word from Dr. Ammon.

"I don't know."

"This is insane," Simon announced. "Lacy, call the
police right now."

"I can't."

"Can't? Why not?"

"He told me not to make any calls."

"And how would he know if you made any calls?"

"Because he's following us."

I swiveled in my seat, nearly giving myself whip-lash. There were several vehicles behind us, but I couldn't make out any of the drivers.

"What does he want?" Simon asked. "Why does he want us to go to the clinic?"

Nurse Bell didn't answer right away and I finally turned to look at her. She stared at me in the mirror.

"Lacy, I am not getting off this road unless you tell me what he wants."

"He wants Lana," she finally admitted.

My blood seemed to turn cold and freeze inside my veins. Simon didn't seem surprised.

"No, I won't do it. Not unless you call the police. Put it on speaker, he can't see you if it's in your lap."

"Simon, please. I don't care if he takes me, but I can't let him hurt Ella. Take me to the clinic, I'll go with him, then you can go to the police and find Ella." Simon opened his mouth and I knew he would start to protest so I placed my hand on his arm and spoke before he could. "Please," I begged.

The muscles in Simon's jaw bunched and rolled. He made a low growling sound before he flipped on his blinker and took the exit Nurse Bell had indicated.

I rested my forehead against the back of his seat and closed my eyes.

"Thank you," I breathed.

The car rolled to a stop and I heard the blinker again:

click, click, click. It seemed loud in the otherwise silent space. The car accelerated and turned. I looked up to watch where we were going.

The road curved through three miles of residential neighborhoods before taking us through franchise alley-the name I gave to the section of any suburb where the road was lined on either side with every fast-food joint, five minute oil change and dollar store you could find in every town across the U.S.

Simon kept glancing in the rearview mirror, watching for Dr. Ammon's vehicle I assumed, and then checking on me. We rode in silence, each lost in our own thoughts. I, for one, wondered for the thousandth time what this guy wanted with me.

For better or worse, I didn't have to wait too long to find out.

About ten minutes later, Simon pulled into the parking lot of the free clinic. The lot overflowed with tiny electric and solar powered cars. A crowd milled around the entrance waiting to go into the packed waiting room.

Simon circled the parking lot twice, deliberately avoiding the only spot that had two spaces open side by side. He finally squeezed into a single space along the west wall of the building. I was grateful for the few extra seconds it would give me to compose myself before I had to face my least favorite person on the planet.

Nurse Bell opened her door and slipped out of the vehicle. She moved up to the sidewalk to give me space to get out. I hesitated and Simon turned to face me.

"Are you sure you want to do this?" he asked.

"I have to," I replied. "At least this time someone knows where I am." Before I lost my nerve, I pushed the passenger seat forward and worked my way awkwardly across the seat and through the sliver of space between the door frame and the back of the seat.

I joined Nurse Bell on the sidewalk and together we watched another car pull into the middle of the double space which Simon had passed by.

"It looks like there are two people," I stated.

"Yes it does," Nurse Bell replied.

"Let's wait at the entrance, near the crowd," Simon suggested once he'd joined us.

Nurse Bell nodded and led the way.

Simon took my hand and we fell in behind her side by side.

My grip on his hand tightened suddenly. Two men stepped out of the car. One was Dr. Ammon, the other was Rafael.

"Lana," Nurse Bell stopped and she said my name.

"I see," I replied.

"Who's the other guy?" Simon asked.

"That's Rafael," Nurse Bell replied.

"The one that-" he stopped and looked at me. I nodded. His lips pressed together into a thin line and his nostrils flared. "I'm going with you."

I didn't respond. Both of Rafael's eyes were black from the bridge of his nose outward and his right ear was bandaged and taped against the side of his head.

"Is that your handiwork?" Simon asked.

I nodded in response.

"Good," he replied.

One corner of my mouth twitched but the smile died before it could reach my eyes when I saw Rafael watching me.

We waited just at the edge of the crowd. Dr. Ammon smiled before he stopped a few feet away from me. He looked completely comfortable.

"Lana, it's so good to see you." He even managed to sound sincere.

I didn't bother to respond.

"What do you want?" Simon demanded.

Dr. Ammon's eyes shifted to Simon and his head tilted slightly.

"Simon Suso, twenty-eight years old, graduate of Maine State University and Senior Resident at Portland's Main Medical Center, why do you care?" Dr. Ammon glanced down at our intertwined fingers, paused deliberately, then shifted back up to Simon's face.

Simon looked a bit flushed, but otherwise unaffected by Dr. Ammon's attempt at intimidation.

"I won't let you hurt her."

Dr. Ammon ignored Simon and shifted his attention to me. "Lana, we each have something the other wants. If you come with me, inside, I might be willing to discuss a trade."

"I'm going with her." Simon stepped toward Dr. Ammon causing Rafael to take a step toward Simon.

Dr. Ammon placed a hand on Rafael's arm.

"Just Miss Wexler I'm afraid. The two of you can wait here and my assistant will keep you company."

Simon glanced back at me, Nurse Bell placed a hand on my shoulder. I nodded.

Dr. Ammon gestured for me to lead the way.

Reluctantly, I disentangled my fingers from Simon's and stepped behind him to avoid getting any closer to Rafael. Dr. Ammon was cold and heartless but, so far, not violent. I felt like I could hold my own against him.

With a deep breath and a long exhale I made my way to the main entrance. Pausing, I cast one final glance back at Simon and Nurse Bell before stepping into a wedge of the rotating doorway.

As I proceeded into the lobby, the press of bodies and cloying stench of sickness assaulted my senses. I stood, frozen, until Dr. Ammon's hand pushed against my back, forcing me toward the receptionist's desk.

We waited for a full minute, watching the receptionist's fingers dance across her keyboard as she expertly ignored us, before Dr. Ammon tapped on the glass.

The middle-aged woman, who looked like she had grown out of, or perhaps into, her chair, glanced up. Her face conveyed weary annoyance, until she recognized Dr. Ammon. Her features quickly shifted to surprise. She sat up straight and slid one half of the glass window aside.

"Dr. Ammon," she said, her voice matched her wide-eyed countenance. "How can I help you?"

"I need to use room 207," he stated in a way that sounded like the woman should have known this.

"Uh, one moment please." The receptionist half-turned and pressed the ear bud in her ear, then spoke into the attached microphone which curved around in front of her mouth. "Hey KellyAnn, Dr. Ammon is here and needs to use room 207." Pause. "Okay." Another pause. "Okay, one second."

The receptionist turned her attention back to Dr. Ammon and lowered the microphone slightly.

"I'm sorry, Doctor, but every room is in use right now. If you go to the second floor waiting room, KellyAnn will let you know as soon as that room becomes available.

Dr. Ammon's anger was not the explosive kind. It was cold and frightening, the kind of anger that gave you goosebumps while you waited to see what he would do.

The receptionist felt it too. Dr. Ammon never said a word, but she seemed to shrink into herself just before the Doctor stepped away from the window and directed me toward the stairwell.

I wondered if there was an elevator, and if so, why Dr. Ammon didn't use it. Was he one of those people that always took the stairs or was it simply to get away from the crowd a few feet earlier.

He followed as I ascended the stairs, all the way to the second level landing. Once we reached the landing, he stepped beside me and gripped my arm just above the elbow before he twisted the knob of the second floor door.

The Doctor directed me to the left, even though a sign clearly indicated the lobby was located to our right. I frowned, but I didn't have to wait long to learn his intentions.

Dr. Ammon steered me toward room 207 and kept a firm grip on my arm. He stopped and knocked on the door before entering a code in the keypad on the wall. The light above the door turned green and he pushed it open.

A young man looked up from his phone, eyes wide and one index finger still poised over the screen.

"I have an emergency and I'm going to have to ask you to leave. Please return to the reception desk and let KellyAnn know you need a new room."

"Dude, I've been waiting for two hours-"

"Unless you'd rather become a live specimen for my research, I suggest you move, now."

The young man blinked twice, then hopped off the elevated seat and hurried out of the room.

Dr. Ammon released my arm and nodded toward the now vacant patient chair. He paused and closed the door.

I have to admit, I was kind in awe of the calm authority the man wielded seemingly without thought or effort. How does a person achieve that kind of confidence?

Maybe by believing he's God, I thought. I watched him open a cabinet and push the contents of the shelf to one side to reveal a small safe deposit box built into the wall.

He pressed his thumb against a scanner and waited for the automatic security system to wake up. After the light turned green, Dr. Ammon held his hand palm out in front of the reflective black panel. After about five seconds the door of the safe deposit box popped open.

A tray of vials and two small cases became visible when Dr. Ammon turned and placed the items on a tray. He left them there, and left me wondering what might be inside those cases. After he'd locked the safe, he hid the door by shifting the items back to their original places in the cabinet. He seemed to take his time arranging things just so, and then moved two steps over to wash his hands in the deep, narrow sink.

My palms began to sweat.

After he dried his hands, he began to pull on a pair of surgical gloves.

"What are you planning to do?"

"Well, Miss Wexler, you've seriously complicated matters by running away from my research facility. Had you stayed where you belonged, this could have been a very gradual process. Now we no longer have that luxury." He unzipped the cases and began to set out an assortment of tools, the sight of which made my stomach start to flip-flop.

I watched him lay out a long, hollow syringe, a tiny but wicked looking scalpel, and a pair of tweezers. There was also the standard gauze, disinfectant, and tube of sealant.

"You didn't answer my question." I was thankful that my voice didn't quaver as much as my heart at that moment.

"I'm going to take blood and tissue samples," he stated. "I need your DNA."

My brow knit into a maze of creases.

"Why?"

Dr. Ammon paused and actually made eye contact with me. He seemed...excited.

"You, my dear, hold the key to our future. Your DNA is naturally resistant to environmental pollutants. It had to happen sooner or later, in order for our species to survive."

The creases in my forehead remained but Dr. Ammon couldn't see them. He'd returned to his preparations.

"What are you talking about?"

"Your DNA, your genetic make-up, it helps you resist endocrine disrupting chemicals and pollution. You have enhanced ability to absorb nutrients from our nutrient-diminished foods. You are one of the few women who can carry a full-term pregnancy. I believe you have passed a portion of this to your daughter, but not in full. If I can find a way to replicate it, you could be responsible for saving our species or, at least, allowing me to."

He actually smiled then, the first genuine smiled I'd ever seen from him.

All the pieces clicked into place, finally.

"You mean Ella has these...abilities...as well."

Dr. Ammon grew quiet.

"You were never treating her, you were experimenting on her!"

"I was determining her types of resistance. She has *some* of your *abilities*, but also has some sensitivities that you do not." As he explained this he wrapped a stretchy band around my arm above the elbow and swabbed the vein.

"You're not going to harm her. You can't afford to." My eyes never left his face and I saw his jaw tense briefly. His eyes remained downcast while he prepared a syringe. "And you're certainly not going to kill me, at least, not without your samples."

Dr. Ammon turned, holding a syringe in a three-fingered grip, and said nothing.

Without thinking, I cocked my arm and slammed my fist into the side of his face.

He stumbled backward into the tray. Glass shattered

and metal clattered as he and his accoutrements fell to the ground. I jumped from the table and opened the door, slamming it behind me before he regained his footing.

A nurse leaned over the reception desk and peered down the hall. I bolted for the stairs and half slid down the railing, clearing three steps at a time.

Heads turned when I burst onto the first floor. I dashed through the crowded waiting room, dodging bodies and wheelchairs.

"Hold on there! Ma'am! Come back here!" The receptionist's voice faded once the rotating doors closed behind me and then spit me out on the other side.

I ducked behind a group of bystanders, peering around and hoping not to be seen by Rafael. What I saw was Simon and Nurse Bell surrounded by the police. Rafael was nowhere to be seen.

Indecision raged within me. The police could help. I wanted to tell them the whole story, everything that happened from the moment I left Cliff Island, but there would be questions, and paperwork, and I didn't have time. Ella needed me.

I ducked behind a car just as the group turned and moved toward the hospital entrance. As they walked, one of the squad cars became visible and I saw Rafael in the back seat of that car.

But he'd driven here in *his* car.

I pulled the clear disc out of my pocket which contained his ID chip. In a half-bent position, I scurried to hide behind the rear of the vehicle and searched the parking lot.

I could hear Nurse Bell's voice. She continued to explain the situation to the police. I waited for the pop and scrape of the revolving door before I rose slightly and crept down the line until I'd reached the driver's side door of Rafael's vehicle.

Carefully, I opened the disc and with the nails of my left thumb and forefinger I removed Rafael's ID. I held the chip in front of the scanner and grinned when I heard the tell-tale snick of the lock releasing.

Trying to be as inconspicuous as possible, I opened the door just enough to squeeze through and slide into the driver's seat. My nostrils flared when I closed the door and inhaled the all too familiar mixture of sport-scented deodorant and hair gel that would haunt my dreams for years, the entirely repellant smell of Rafael.

After placing Rafael's ID chip against the sensor on the steering wheel, I covered it with my left palm and gripped tight to keep it in place. With my right index finger, I pressed the engine start button. The car revved to life and, to my astonishment, classical music drifted from the radio.

Really not what I'd expected either of them to listen to.

I turned off the radio and glanced at the clock, 12:45. I could still make that one o'clock appointment with Dr. Myers. With any luck the police would delay Dr. Ammon long enough that she wouldn't know what had happened until it was too late.

Something told me Ella was in that hospital and I intended to find her.

CHAPTER 17

AFTER PUTTING THE car in auto, I programmed the route to The Main Memorial Hospital. The vehicle backed itself out of the parking space and I couldn't help but glance toward the squad car which held Rafael. Fortunately, I didn't have a clear view of him. I hoped he couldn't see me, or his car, pulling away.

High on adrenaline and anxious as hell is no way to enter east coast traffic. On Cliff Island we didn't even have cars and in college I'd always been able to find a ride, or take public transportation. I said a silent pray of thanks for auto-drive but still gripped the steering wheel until my knuckles turned white. The electric mini wove in and out of traffic to make the one'o'clock arrival time I'd pre-programmed.

I finally exhaled when the car pulled into a parking space on level twelve of the hospital's parking garage.

My shaking hands released the steering wheel and opened the driver's side door. I climbed out of the car into the heart of the poorly lit concrete monstrosity. I felt small and, at the same time, conspicuous as my footfalls echoed through the windowless structure.

The clear case with Rafael's ID found a home in one of the inner pockets of the hooded jacket I'd borrowed from the backseat of the car. I took the elevator to the main floor then followed the yellow arrows to the primary receiving area.

"Hello, how may I help you?" A short-haired round-faced woman greeted me. I approached her territory. Her name tag identified her as Mia, no surname included.

"Hi," I replied. "I have a one 'o'clock appointment with Dr. Myers."

"Okay, one moment please." Mia's long and perfectly manicured nails clicked against the screen of her monitor. She tapped icons in a flurry of motion, making me very conscious of my own chewed and broken fingernails. I curled my hands into loose fists while I waited.

"Name please," Mia stated. The rhythmic clicking paused as she waited for my response.

"Lana Wexler." My voice sounded resigned. I'd considered giving Nurse Bell's name, but I'd be found out the moment someone scanned my ID.

A few more clicks of the screen and then Mia looked up with a smile.

"Dr. Myers is expecting you. Just scan your ID at those double doors, go straight through to the patient elevators and take one to the fourth floor. Go to the nurse's desk on that level to find out which room you'll be in."

"Thank you."

Mia nodded and smiled, then shifted her attention to the next person in line.

Swallowing my fear, I marched toward the double doors and held my hand up to the scanner. The doors slid apart. I proceeded forward, and doubts began to creep in. *What if Ella isn't here? What will I say to Dr. Myers? How will I find Ella? What if Dr. Ammon had called Dr. Myers already? What if Ella isn't here?*

Like a broken record that I couldn't turn off, the questions spun through my mind. When I finally stepped off the elevator onto the fourth floor, I felt like I'd slammed a coffee and all-day energy combined. My arms and legs quivered, my heart pounded, and I couldn't calm my mind enough to focus on a single thought.

The nurse's desk stood kitty-corner to the elevator, but at the moment, no-one was there. I glanced from the desk down the long hallway.

Rooms lined either side of the corridor. Small windows were built into the top of each door. After one more glance at the desk to confirm no one had materialized, I hurried past and stopped at the first door. I stood on my tip-toes to peer into the window and found it empty. Natural light from the outer windows illuminated the perfectly made bed and OCD-induced organization of the room.

A very pregnant woman who looked to be in her early thirties occupied the second room.

My mouth had gone dry and I could actually hear my heart pounding. I hurried across the hall to the third door.

When I looked into that window, I gasped and pressed my hand to the clear pane.

A voluptuous woman rocked back and forth in a rocking chair staring down at the baby sleeping peacefully in the crook of her arm.

"Ella," my voice broke as I said her name and then my vision began to blur.

After dashing the tears from my eyes, I knocked lightly on the window, conscious of the sleeping baby, *my* sleeping baby. I watched as the woman I could only assume was Marjorie, looked up.

Our eyes met for a split second before mine returned to my daughter.

My fingers continued to tap like a reflex I could not stop and the tears began again. I was only semi-aware of Marjorie rising and approaching the door. It took all my effort to remain on my feet but I couldn't take my eyes off my Ella. She was so big! Her hair had grown and she'd gained weight. Her face was full and round and perfect.

When the door zipped open, the weight which had been pressed against it suddenly had nothing to support it. I stumbled forward and would have fallen if Marjorie hadn't reached out with one arm to catch me.

I heard the door close behind me as I regained my balance.

"Thank you, I'm sorry, I…" My voice cut off. I stood and found myself inches away from my baby girl.

Without even thinking, I reached for her. Marjorie placed her in my arms.

A grin stretched across my face. I began to laugh and

cry at the same time. I wanted desperately to squeeze her and kiss her, but she looked so calm, so peaceful, I didn't want to wake her up. So I stood like a statue, afraid to move. I felt like I'd forgotten how to hold my own child.

Two strong hands gripped my shoulders and guided me toward the rocking chair. Grateful, I sat, stared at my daughter through the flood of tears, and grinned until my cheeks began to hurt.

She was safe. She was healthy. My daughter was here, in my arms, and she was safe.

Several minutes passed before I finally whispered, "This is my daughter."

I'd mostly been thinking out loud, trying to confirm that this moment was real. I was almost surprised when Marjorie responded.

"I can see that," she replied.

I looked up, having heard the sadness in her voice. I could see it too, in the lines of her young face. She appeared to be my age, but her eyes looked older.

"They told me you had died, complications during delivery."

I nodded, and then replied, "They took her from me."

Marjorie looked up and away. I could see her throat working, her eyes blinking fast.

"Thank you, Marjorie isn't it? Ella looks so healthy, and so happy. Thank you for taking care of her."

Marjorie's eyes closed for a moment, and she did cry then, just two tears, one from each eye that she didn't bother to wipe away before she looked back at me.

"My baby was stillborn. A baby boy."

"I'm so sorry," I responded, feeling fresh tears fill my eyes. "What was his name?"

A hint of a smile pulled at one corner of her mouth.

"Jameson Ray," she replied. She paused a moment, then added, "You know, you're the first person to ask me that."

"I'm sorry about all of this, that you had to be involved, it must be like losing him all over again," I said softly, nodding toward Ella.

Marjorie took a deep breath and shook her head.

"She was never mine. Not that I didn't fall in love with her mind you, but I knew she wasn't meant for me." Marjorie paused and her brow furrowed slightly. "I think the Doctor meant to keep her."

I stopped rocking and felt a cold chill creep down my neck and spread through my arms.

"Dr. Ammon?" I asked.

Marjorie's eyebrows pulled together and she shook her head. "No, Dr. Myers."

Ella must have felt my tension, because she began to stir. In response I began rocking again, but she became increasingly fussy.

"I think she's hungry," Marjorie said. "This is typically when she eats."

"Oh," I replied. "I, uh…" I glanced from Ella to Marjorie. "Could you?"

Marjorie nodded and we traded places. She settled into the rocking chair and expertly shifted Ella into position to nurse once I handed her over. Ella attached herself to Marjorie and immediately calmed.

I could have wept then, for all that they had taken from me. I couldn't even feed my own daughter. Instead of tears, a new kind of rage began to burn through me. *How could they do this? How could they use us like this without expecting to answer for it?*

"How did you end up on Dr. Ammon's island?" I asked, wondering if she had also been "referred" by Dr. Myers.

"I volunteered," Marjorie replied. "I'd lost two babies already, and then lost my husband while I was pregnant with the third. I thought they might be able to help." She glanced down at Ella, who continued to nurse with her eyes open, watching Marjorie.

"Oh, Marjorie, I'm so sorry." Sorry seemed woefully inadequate in the face of her loss, but I didn't know what else to say.

Marjorie just nodded slowly, then sighed and said, "Me too. Me too."

I jumped and turned when I heard the door zip open behind me.

Goosebumps rose along my suddenly cold arms when Dr. Myers entered the room. She glanced from me to Ella and back again.

"Miss Wexler, it's so good to see you." She nodded toward my hand. "I see you already acquired a new ID." The tone of her voice was casual…too casual. She didn't ask me what I was doing in Marjorie's room, or how I'd gotten in, she was fishing for answers to different questions.

For the moment I had a slight advantage. I decided to force her hand.

"No, I got the old one back...from your *husband's* office." I watched her face closely. She was good. She couldn't quite suppress the slight widening of her eyes and an almost imperceptible flaring of her nostrils, but aside from these small tells, her expression remained neutral.

"I see," she replied calmly. "Why don't we talk about this in my office?"

"No, I'm not leaving my daughter." Again I saw her glance to Ella. This time her jaw tightened and she faced me. "Whatever you have to say, Marjorie deserves to hear it as well, since you're using her too."

Dr. Myers pulled her shoulders back and folded her hands in front of her.

"Dr. Ammon leads the world in cutting edge research on reproduction, pre and post-natal child development, and the effects of environmental influences. What he does, he does for the good of us all. I'm certain you've misinterpreted his actions."

I laughed, a full, spontaneous, from the gut laugh that just couldn't be held in.

"Misinterpreted?" I exclaimed once I'd regained my breath. "I guess a jury will have to decide just how many of his actions I've *misinterpreted*."

Dr. Myers's eyes narrowed.

"In case you didn't know, your husband and his assistant are already in custody, and I fully intend to press charges."

The Doctor tipped her head to the side slightly. She

slid her hands into the big pockets on the front of her long white lab coat.

"But how will you press charges, Lana? You're dead."

Dr. Myers stepped forward and simultaneously reached for my arm. The fingers of her left hand circled my forearm and pulled me closer before I could react and start to pull away.

With her right hand she withdrew a syringe from one of those deep pockets and I pulled with all my strength.

We stumbled together for several steps. She still had a grip on my arm, but was off balance enough that she couldn't get her syringe into position.

Something solid connected with my ribcage and I glanced back to see the bed railing pressed into my side. The bed itself blocked any additional backward movement.

I grabbed for her right wrist with my left hand. We struggled like that, locked together, oblivious to anything around us, until I caught a flash of movement and heard a thunk. Something solid connected with the back of Dr. Myers's skull.

She released her grip on my wrist and she slid to the floor, nearly pulling me down with her until I had the presence of mind to let go of her.

After I'd regained my footing, I looked at Marjorie. She stood a few feet away, baby in one arm, metal tray turned weapon in the other.

"Thank you."

Marjorie nodded. We both jumped when the door zipped open again. This time, four police officers poured into the room, followed by Nurse Bell and Simon.

Nurse Bell rushed to me and wrapped her arms around me.

"You're okay! I'm so glad you're okay!" Nurse Bell released me and turned to Marjorie. She gasped. "It's Ella! You found Ella!"

Simon walked to my side and squeezed my hand. I smiled up at him.

One of the police officers approached and nodded.

"Miss Wexler?"

I nodded in return.

"I realize you've been through a lot today, but I'm going to have to ask you to come with me." Then he turned to address Marjorie. "Both of you."

Marjorie and I nodded simultaneously.

I reached for Ella and Marjorie placed her in my arms. She'd fallen asleep again.

"She's beautiful," Simon said softly.

I grinned and nodded, feeling whole again for the first time in weeks.

A second officer snapped pictures of the room, including Dr. Myers who still lay in a heap on the floor.

"What happened?" Nurse Bell asked.

The first officer watched me, waiting in anticipation of my response.

"Well, I saw Ella through the window and knocked. Marjorie let me in. We talked for a few minutes then Dr. Myers came in. She wanted me to go with her but I refused. Eventually she tried to inject whatever is in that syringe," I nodded toward the syringe which a woman with gloves on was retrieving from the floor and placing in a baggie, "into me. I was trying to fight her off and then Marjorie…helped me. That's about it."

The officer nodded and clicked the end of what I'd thought was a pen. He caught my expression and held the device out for me to see.

"Voice recorder," he explained.

I nodded.

"Did you get Dr. Ammon?" I asked.

"Yep," Nurse Bell responded. "We caught him on the stairwell. At first we thought he was running away, but figured out he was trying to catch you. What did you do?"

I glanced over at the officer's voice recorder.

"It's a long story. Let's save it for the station."

We were escorted out of the building to the waiting squad car.

"Uh, what about a car seat? We don't have a car seat."

"We already borrowed one from the hospital." The officer smiled and he held open the door.

Marjorie and I squeezed into the back seat with Ella's car seat. Nurse Bell slid into the front.

"I'll follow and meet you there," Simon stated. "Will you be okay?"

"Yeah, I think I will." I nodded. I adjusted Ella in her seat, and then turned to Marjorie and asked, "Will you be okay?"

Marjorie pressed her lips together and the corners of her mouth quirked upward as she patted my arm. "Don't you worry about me."

CHAPTER 18

AFTER THE POLICE recorded my full story and got all their questions answered, they asked if I would be able to stay close in order to testify at Dr. Ammon's trial.

"You're welcome to stay with me," Marjorie offered. "It's a small place, my sister and niece live there too, but you'd have lots of help, just until you feel comfortable on your own."

I threw my free arm around Marjorie's neck and hugged her kind of sideways so as not to crush Ella.

"Thank you, Marjorie," I breathed. "That would be perfect."

It would also give Marjorie a little more time with Ella. I knew she was trying to be strong for my sake, but it was clear she wasn't ready to let Ella go, not yet.

Simon and Nurse Bell waited in the lobby. They stood as Marjorie and I walked out and we all paused. Everyone seemed to be wondering what to do next.

"Well, I think I'm the only one with a car here. Why don't I drive you all home?"

Simon suggested.

"Do you have to work tonight?" Nurse Bell asked.

"I called in. I haven't slept since you arrived yesterday so I don't think I could make it through another shift."

Nurse Bell cocked an eyebrow.

"In that case, maybe I should drive everyone home in your car."

Simon nodded, "Good idea."

Marjorie held up a hand and said, "My sister's here to pick me up. The police called her. Thank you for the offer though." She paused and focused on me. "I'll see you at the house?"

I nodded and we all waved. Marjorie turned and was immediately sandwiched in a crushing hug between her sister and her niece.

The police provided us with a car seat. I slid into the back seat of Simon's car and buckled Ella in. Exhaustion pressed down on me like a ton of seawater. I nodded once I was certain that Ella was secure, and within seconds my eyes were closed.

"Lana." A distant voice called my name, a voice that seemed at once a part of a dream and an all-too vivid reality. "Lana, time to wake up."

A hand gripped my shoulder and slid me gently from side to side.

My eyelids felt like they'd been sewn shut, they just did not want to open. Finally, I managed a big enough slit that I could see Simon's face staring at me from the front seat.

I closed my mouth, which I realized had been hanging slightly open, blinked a few times and checked on Ella. She slept peacefully beside me.

Next I glanced out the window.

"Where are we?" I asked.

"Marjorie's apartment," Simon replied. "That's where you're staying, right?"

"Oh, yeah."

Slowly I began to return to the land of the living. I unbuckled and checked around to make sure I had everything off the floor and seats, then I unhooked Ella's seat and reached for the door handle.

"Here, wait, let me help."

As Simon bolted from his seat and dashed around the car, I paused and smiled. After he'd opened the passenger door, I handed Ella out in her seat then maneuvered my way under the strap and around the front seat until I finally stood facing Simon.

"This looks like a pretty small apartment for five people. If it gets too crowded here, or maybe when the trial is done, I uh...well, there's an extra room at my place."

With a smile I reached up and rested my hand against Simon's cheek.

"Thank you. That is really sweet of you. For now I need some help with Ella, and Marjorie needs some time too. She's lost so much," I sighed and continued. "I think when this is all done, I want to go home." Simon's shoulders sagged a little. I smiled and added, "But you know, my parents' old house has an outbuilding that would be perfect for a small clinic. The island could really use its own Doctor."

Simon's eyes lit up and the corners of his mouth curved upwards.

"Sounds interesting. I've always loved islands."

I grinned and had just begun to contemplate leaning in for a kiss when I heard someone call my name.

I turned and saw Marjorie's niece waving and running across the parking lot.

"Kali May you get back here!" her mother called from the doorway.

"I'm just gonna help!" she called back, not even slowing down until she came to full stop in front of me. "Can I help?"

I laughed and took a step away from Simon.

"Sure," I replied. "I've got a couple of bags in the back. I could use a hand with those."

We'd made a stop to retrieve my belongings, and Nurse Bell had loaded a bag with all the clothes she could find that might fit me.

Simon popped the trunk and Kali and I each pulled out a suitcase.

"That's it?" she asked, peering into corners of the tiny storage space.

"That's it for now. I need to get some more things for Ella-"

"Oooh, can I help? Can I pick out some outfits for her?"

I laughed again and Simon smiled.

"Looks like you're going to have a surplus of help," Simon remarked.

Kali led the way back to the apartment, Simon brought up the rear with Ella swinging in her seat. Kali's mother scowled at her as she entered the apartment, but quickly smoothed her features and then gave me a welcoming grin.

"Come on in. I'll show you to your room."

I followed through the living room and down a short hallway which only had three doors. Marjorie was already in the room cleaning and arranging things, she'd already set up a bedside basinet.

"Is this your room? I can't kick you out of your own room!"

"You're not kicking me out. I asked you to stay. I've got a cot and you and the baby need a quiet place, well, as quiet as it can get around here." She cocked an eyebrow at her niece who'd followed us into the room and giggled at Marjorie's teasing.

"Again, thank you."

Marjorie nodded.

"Make yourself comfortable. I'll go make something to eat and you, little helper, can come with me."

"But I-"

Marjorie shooed Kali out of the room. I could hear her protesting all the way to the kitchen.

Simon set Ella's seat down on the floor and turned to face me.

"You have my number, right? Call me anytime and let me know if there's anything I can do to help. I would love to see you, and Ella, anytime." Simon fiddled with his watch, clearly stalling.

Truth be told, I didn't want him to leave either. It seemed strange how quickly I'd come to count on him being there.

"Simon, I can't thank you enough, for helping us, and…for everything."

He reached for my hand and when I took his, he squeezed gently, and then he stepped forward and placed his other hand on my shoulder. He leaned closer and my heart started to race.

What began as a sweet, soft, goodbye kiss turned into something far more urgent. Our hands came untwined so that we could wrap our arms around each other until no space remained between our bodies.

A year's worth of pent-up emotion seemed to release in that kiss.

Then Ella started to cry.

We pulled apart reluctantly, breathlessly. I moved to unbuckle Ella from her seat, attempting to gather my scattered wits.

"Um, I think she might be hungry. I'm going to have to take her to Marjorie until we can get a pump and some bottles."

I tried to simultaneously bounce and pat Ella's back as I carried her down the hall.

"Marjorie?" I said once we'd reached the kitchen. "I think she's hungry."

Marjorie glanced at the clock then walked over and hooked a finger in the back of Ella's pants and pulled both clothes and diaper out far enough that she could peek down inside.

"Nope, she needs to be changed."

I felt awful that I hadn't thought of that.

Marjorie chuckled.

"Nobody's born a perfect parent, you learn as you go, and you learn from your mistakes. The most important thing is that you love her. The rest is just details."

I smiled and nodded. I half-turned and then realized I didn't have any diapers.

"Uh, do you have any diapers?"

"Yep, I had the room all stocked up for my boy. They're in the top dresser drawer. There's a changing pad too, on top of the dresser."

"Oh, thank you." I felt awful that I would be using the items meant for her son.

Marjorie noticed my look and smiled.

"I'm glad they're being used. It would be so much worse if they just sat in that room, staring at me until I worked up the nerve to get rid of 'em."

I smiled my gratitude and turned to Simon.

He pulled his phone from his pocket and held it up, poised to type.

"Marjorie, can I put in your home number? And then I'll be out of your hair."

Marjorie told him and he typed, then shoved his phone back in his pocket.

"All right, I'll get going, please call if you need any-thing." He waved to Marjorie, and then smiled at me. "Bye, Lana."

"Bye, Simon. Thank you."

He nodded and ducked out the front door as Ella's wails intensified.

Once Ella had been changed and fed, I laid her on the bed, curled up next to her and just watched her until we both fell asleep. For the first time in what seemed like forever I slept a deep, dreamless sleep with my daughter's tiny hand curled around my fingers.

CHAPTER 19

THE NEXT WEEKS passed in a blur. I tried to put my life back together while simultaneously serving as a witness for a criminal trial. I finally got a new phone. I called a few close friends and co-workers to let them know that I was, in fact, not dead. Evelyn nearly had a heart attack. She even woke Ella when she screeched the news to James.

She had a lot of questions that I couldn't answer yet, not until the trial was over. The best I could do was send a picture of Ella and promise to tell her the whole story as soon as I got home.

Within minutes of saying goodbye to Evelyn, my phone began to ring and beep and buzz like a one man band on steroids. I finally had to turn it off so that Ella and I could get some sleep.

I spent the majority of the trial in a separate room at the courthouse, watching the proceedings on a live-stream feed. I learned that Dr. Ammon and Dr. Myers had been trying to have a baby for years, and had lost four along the way. That explained a lot. They had the perfect combination of genius and desperation to make what had started as legitimate and necessary research twist into a dangerous obsession.

Dr. Myers confessed that when she'd seen the results of my first blood test, she saw a perfect opportunity to solve both of their problems at once. She wanted a baby, Dr. Ammon wanted to discover the "cure" for our world's rapidly declining population. It all would have worked out perfectly for them if I hadn't escaped.

I could almost sympathize with them.

When it was my turn to appear in court, Marjorie stayed with Ella in our private room. I began to sweat and get goose bumps all at the same time. I followed the constable to the courtroom.

Neither Dr. Ammon nor Dr. Myers made eye contact with me. I took a deep breath and steeled myself for an interrogation, quite confident that no matter how the lawyers might try to twist my words, I was in the right.

The majority of my account went unchallenged. The defense attorney asked a few questions for clarification, prompted me at times to flesh out my account. I began to relax when I was allowed to speak without being attacked.

Imagine my surprise when I was presented with a document, signed by my own hand, that gave permission for Dr. Ammon to conduct his experiments. Of course they weren't called "experiments" on the actual piece of paper. They were referred to as "exploratory medical procedures to determine the child's response and/or resistance to any medical treatments deemed necessary."

There wasn't much I could say to defend myself there.

"I never gave him permission to steal my child."

"No further questions, your honor."

I was escorted out, shaking now with rage, rage that abated quickly once Ella was back in my arms. Whatever happened to them was out of my control. I would not waste any more of my energy on them. I needed it all for Ella.

The trial was supposed to be closed so, naturally, the news of the proceedings had gone viral. Quite a crowd gathered outside the courthouse to hear the final verdict.

I was in our private room, sitting down, when I heard the Dr. Myers declared "not guilty" on three counts and Dr. Ammon "not guilty" on two. When they had worked their way down the list to kidnapping, attempted murder, and falsifying legal records, I finally heard the word "guilty".

Marjorie smiled and nodded. I felt tension drain from my body.

We were released by a court official and Marjorie guided me from the quiet room into a world of flashing lights and shouting voices.

I felt a pair of strong arms wrap around me and I leaned into Simon's embrace.

"Lana, congratulations!" Nurse Bell followed closely behind Simon and grinned in a mixture of excitement and relief.

"I can't thank all of you enough, and you," I said. I stepped out of Simon's arms to hug Nurse Bell. "You saved us."

Nurse Bell shrugged and waved it off.

"Just send me pictures once in a while, all right."

I smiled and nodded. "I will."

Nurse Bell's eyes narrowed suddenly and her eyes fixed on some point behind me. I turned and followed her gaze.

A woman in a pencil skirt and matching blazer approached, followed closely by a balding man in a designer suit and a power tie.

I turned to face them. They stopped an arm's length away.

"Miss Wexler, on behalf of the Academy of Medical Research, we wish to extend our apologies and deepest sympathies for all that you've endured. I hope you know that the actions of these two individuals were carried out without our knowledge or consent." She paused and watched my face.

"I understand. Apology accepted. Thank you." My response was clipped and cold, the woman nodded, then pressed her fingertips together in front of her and prepared to speak again.

I knew what was coming.

"The research itself is critically important and, had it been conducted with your full knowledge and consent, could be the greatest discovery of our time." She paused again, when I did not respond, she continued. "We would like to invite you, when and if you are ready, to help us solve the reproduction crisis."

Simon placed a hand on my shoulder and began to move forward, trying to block me from the woman's view.

I placed a hand on his arm and shook my head slightly before turning back to address the woman.

"I've given this a lot of thought." I paused. The woman's eyebrows rose in expectation. I swallowed and glanced at Marjorie. "I'm willing to help, not for you and your discovery mind you, but for the families who've suffered the loss of their babies. When I'm ready to help, I'll call you, and it will be on my terms."

The woman grinned and practically vibrated with excitement.

"First, I need some time." I gave the woman and the man behind her a hard look. She schooled her features and nodded gravely. "If possible, I do not wish to return to the mainland, maybe ever. I want all communication and…exchanges…to be handled by Dr. Simon Suso." I motioned to Simon, standing to my right. The woman's eyes followed, then widened slightly, but she nodded.

"Of course, that all sounds very reasonable given your recent experience. Is there anything else?"

"Yes," I replied. "No one touches my daughter."

"Absolutely," she agreed. The woman reached into one front pocket of her blazer and pulled out a business card. "Here's my number," she said, holding the card out to me. "You can have Dr. Suso call us whenever you're ready."

I nodded, took the card, and slid it into my pocket. The woman nodded once more and said, "Again, we're sorry. Thank you for your willingness to listen and perhaps, eventually, help us solve this."

The woman turned and left, the man followed.

I leaned back into Simon and he kissed the top of my head.

"Well, now what?" he asked.

"I want to go home."

Simon drove me to Marjorie's apartment where I packed my things and exchanged tearful goodbyes with Marjorie, Kali, and Anna.

They had become my family, and Ella's. As much as I wanted to go home, I didn't want to leave them.

"What am I going to do without you?" I asked, wrapping Marjorie in a hug.

"You're going to be just fine," Marjorie replied.

"Are you sure you don't want to come? Cliff Island is beautiful, especially in August. Soon the leaves will start to change color. I think you'd like it there."

Marjorie smiled, and then responded, "I'll come to visit, no doubt about that, but I belong here. Besides," she raised her eyebrows and shifted her gaze pointedly from me to Simon and back again. "I have a feeling I'd just be in the way."

I blushed and Simon grinned.

Between the five of us we managed to carry all of my bags, which contained mostly clothes and toys for Ella, out to Simon's little electric car.

"It's a lot more than I came with. Do you think it will all fit?"

"We'll make it fit," Simon declared.

Like a puzzle, Simon found a place for all the pieces, including me and Ella. Not a millimeter of space wasted.

We waved and blew kisses out the window as Simon pulled out of the parking lot.

It took several trips from Simon's house down to his boat. By the time we were all loaded up, my legs quivered with fatigue.

Simon lowered the boat into the water and we took off. The rocking motion of the small but sea-worthy craft quickly lulled Ella to sleep. We spent most of the trip in silence. I, for one, reveled in the peace, restored by the sunlight and the spray of salt water. There's something about the vastness of the ocean that manages to make the rest of the world and all of its problems seem small in comparison.

I let the sea rock me in her arms.

As we approached the Cliff Island Harbor, I could see every resident of the island, and possibly every worker from the docks of the sea farm, waiting to welcome us.

Unloading the boat went considerably faster than the loading. There was no lack of helping hands to tie off the boat and haul bags. I simply strapped Ella to me and accepted hug after hug, completely overwhelmed.

The whole island escorted us back to my parent's old house, the one I hadn't spent a night in since their death.

A whole new wave of emotion hit me when I thought of them and how much they would have loved to meet their granddaughter.

I cried when we walked inside and found that the house had been cleaned from top to bottom, opened up to let in the fresh summer breeze, and the fridge had even been stocked with fish and wild blueberry crisp.

My friends were quick to deposit bags and start pulling out food.

Ella began to fuss so I made her a bottle and stole out of the noisy house to an oversized wicker chair on the front porch.

The sound of familiar voices rose and fell in the background. I gazed out at the ocean and inhaled the scent of cold salt, fish, and warm blueberries.

"That's the smell of home, baby girl," I whispered. "We are finally home."

AFTERWORD

THIS NOVEL BEGAN as a short story that I wrote in response to my second pregnancy loss. It was darker and more graphic than anything I'd written before. I tucked the story away and worked on other projects, but I thought about it periodically, and whenever I did, more ideas would evolve. After losing a third baby, I finally decided to develop the idea into a full-length novel. It is not my personal story of course, but I feel like it encompasses a lot of the emotions that I went through during that time.

Throughout the process of grieving and healing and having three full-term healthy pregnancies, I realized that pregnancy loss is just something that people don't talk about much. It's not an easy thing to bring up in conversation. It's not a pleasant memory or story to share with new acquaintances. It may happen before friends or family even know that you are pregnant, so you might feel awkward talking about it. Also, the fact that you never really got to meet or know this little person means there are not a lot of memories or stories of them to share, just the heart-wrenching memory of their loss. Therefore, most people don't know that so many other parents have dealt with the loss of a baby.

Gutted is the best word I could think of to describe what it feels like to lose a child. So, that is what this story is called.

I don't really have any great advice or wise words for the parents who've shared this experience. The one thing that I learned that I can apply equally to each of my situations is that I am not in control. No matter how much I want to be sometimes, I am not. The only thing I can say to others is that you are not alone and your babies are not alone.

ACKNOWLEDGMENTS

THANK YOU so much for reading this story, for giving it, and me, a chance. I hope that you loved it. No matter how you felt about it, I would deeply appreciate if you left a review on Amazon or Goodreads. Reviews help other people discover the book and help them decide if they want to read it.

The ecopolis in the story is based on a design by Vincent Callebaut. I saw the pictures and knew that I needed to incorporate these beautiful images into a science fiction novel. You can follow him on twitter @VCALLEBAUT to see and learn more about his amazing sustainable designs.

Thank you to my wonderful Beta readers this time around: Carrie Aldrich, Owen H., Diane Stone, and Sarah Fox. I can't thank you enough for helping me make this story the best that it could be!

To Robynne at Damonza: a HUGE thank you for the absolutely awesome cover for Gutted. I love it so much! I hope you do too.

I want to give a special thank you and shout out to Hope of The Reader's Review blog. I am so grateful to you for reading all of my books and being excited for more!

ABOUT THE AUTHOR

NICOLE L. BATES is the author of three science fiction adventures, *Empyrean*, *Empyrean's Fall*, and *Emyrean's Future* as well as the sci-fi standalone thriller, *Gutted*. She grew up in Northern Michigan and, after moving seven times, she has once again settled in her home state with her family. You can find out more about Nicole and her work by following Nicole L. Bates on social media or signing up to receive her author newsletter. linktr.ee/ NicoleLBates